the
INWARD JOURNEY

the INWARD JOURNEY

A NOVEL

KATE EVANS

BREAKWATER
P.O. Box 2188, St. John's, NL, Canada, A1C 6E6
www.breakwaterbooks.com

LIBRARY AND ARCHIVES CANADA CATALOGUING IN PUBLICATION
Evans, Kate, 1943-2016, author
The inward journey / Kate Evans.
ISBN 978-1-55081-658-7 (paperback)
I. Title.
PS8609.V338I59 2016   C813'.6   C2016-905777-1
Copyright ©2016 Kate Evans
Cover photo ©Ed Hannon | www.visionsofthepast.ie

We acknowledge the support of the Canada Council for the Arts, which last year invested
$153 million to bring the arts to Canadians throughout the country. We acknowledge the
financial support of the Government of Canada and the Government of Newfoundland
and Labrador through the Department of Business, Tourism, Culture and Rural
Development for our publishing activities. PRINTED AND BOUND IN CANADA.

 Canada Council   Conseil des Arts
for the Arts   du Canada
 Canadä   Newfoundland
Labrador

Breakwater Books is committed to choosing papers and materials for our books that help
to protect our environment. To this end, this book is printed on a recycled paper that is
certified by the Forest Stewardship Council'.

MIX
Paper from
responsible sources
FSC
www.fsc.org   FSC® C004071

*t*his place is getting on my nerves. Today when lunch came things went from bad to worse. The nurse's aide tried to tie a bib around my neck.

"I'm NOT a child," I said, "so don't treat me like one."

She proceeded to go on about my beautiful clothes and what a pity it was to spoil them by "dribbling bits of food." She was trying to be helpful but I was not going to wear a bib! I already told her that.

"There's no shame in losing your sight, girl, but you must wear a bib."

Must! That was the wrong word to use. "Get me a napkin," I said. "That is what civilized people use."

I cannot tolerate this stupidity. She left and came back with a cheap papery thing, which she tried to tuck under my chin. I snatched it away and threw it in a ball on the floor. The plate would have followed if the girl had not anticipated my next move and whisked it away just in time.

At that moment Eleanor, the only nurse around with any sense of decorum, walked into the room.

"I'll handle this," she said, and handed me a small clean towel, set my plate neatly in front of me and left without another word.

This is my reality now. I have become a dribbling, cantankerous old woman. Like a petulant child, I have been unceremoniously reprimanded and have alienated the only person in this place who understands me. I listen for Eleanor's voice in the corridor, recognize her footsteps and sense her crisp presence even if she passes by my door. Now she has left in a huff and things will never be the same.

When that rude nurse's aide returned for my lunch tray, she picked up the knife and fork, which I had laid neatly on my plate, threw them with a loud clatter onto the metal tray, and then under her breath, just loud enough for me to hear, muttered, "Get a life woman." The impudence of the girl. Time was I would have put her in her place but before I could draw a breath she was off out the door.

Get a life indeed! What does she know of life? How it can turn on you in an instant and strike like a viper. What is she suggesting, that I take a walk and pluck another life from a tree like a ripe plum? The airs these people give themselves.

I have ended up in this place, through no fault of my own. I've been singled out, first by God and then by my own flesh and blood. A long finger, like the one at the end of the muscled arm on the ceiling of the Sistine Chapel, points at me — you, you are the one. You are the one to be punished.

That girl, that nurse's aide, she needs to know that I had a life, a life of privilege and position in society, one that she could only dream of. I am, after all, a Bolfe, a woman of breeding. My family comes from the Irish aristocracy. At one time they owned a large estate in the west of Ireland ceded to them in recognition of service to His Majesty the King. My grandmother, Philippa Bolfe, was a proud, determined lady, with a passion for horses. I inherited that passion.

"Sylvia," she would say, "you need spunk to ride a horse like a champion, spunk, to drive forward, straight for the fence, no hesitation, no second guessing, up and over!"

"Mummy says I must be careful and ride like a lady."

"Nonsense. There is nothing wrong with a bit of spunk. Your mother could do with a bit of spunk."

Granny never pronounced her name Balfe in that flat Irish way. She said Bolfe, her cheeks puffing slightly around her small mouth. I thought it gave her a decided air of authority. She insisted that I do the same. When my mother married Edward Carter, "a lout with money" in Granny's estimation, he owned a small stud farm located in the lush horse country of County Kildare. This no doubt sweetened the match between her only daughter and Edward Carter, although she would never acknowledge it. When they married, Granny insisted that Mummy keep her maiden name as part of the deal. "More fitting," she pronounced. So we became known as the Bolfe-Carters.

Whatever has become of Sylvia Bolfe-Carter?

Oh dear! I have upset myself again. Bitterness and regret are creeping back into my life. I have allowed them back, even welcomed them. They have settled in like a pushy neighbour who drops by and refuses to leave.

I wish it would stop raining. It renders my world even more faded and lifeless than it already is. The constant tapping on the windowpane irritates me. Why do I have to be reminded that outside it is raining, that there are endless rivulets of water streaming down the windowpane. That I am close to being totally blind. Yes, damn it. There it is. I am trapped in this chair with nowhere to go. I must now live inside my head fighting a war within myself.

I did become a champion horse woman as Granny wished, and while she lived she was always there to urge me on. One day when I was about eleven, after an exceptional performance at a show, I was summoned to her private sitting room. There was a formality about this request that was slightly unsettling.

Once we were seated, Granny leaned slightly forward to offer guarded, carefully worded praise. "It is important to understand that you show remarkable talent for your age. You have an excellent seat, natural poise, strength and ability beyond your years, though there are areas that need work, which I am confident you can master," she said. "But most of all, and critical to your continued success, is a better horse."

She paused for a moment, assessing my reaction. "I will speak to your father about this but you, my dear, must use your charm to persuade him to buy you a good mount. I intend to suggest that you have one of that new breed of Irish sport horse that are now in demand and causing a stir in equestrian circles around the world."

As she spoke her eyes glittered with determination, they burrowed into me like a laser, held me spellbound in wrapped admiration. "This venture will be costly and as your father is not free with his money we need a strategy." Her eyes demanded that I, in turn, reflect her determination.

"I have heard him talk to the groom about plans to expand the farm. We must appeal to his business sense. Make him feel that your success will put the stud farm here at Kilgraney on the map. Make him feel that it is his idea that it can work. Can you do that?"

I nodded vigorously and kept on nodding. "This is a splendid idea, Granny," I said, breathless at the very thought of a beautiful new horse — one that could meet my growing ambition and boost my tender ego.

"We have a plan then," she said striking the floor with her silver-topped cane. Her secret smile signaled the end of the discussion.

I hugged her with a fierce zeal.

Well I was wrong about Eleanor. She came in again before dinner and handed me a package.

"I've brought you a gift," she said as I undid the package. I was relieved to hear a happy ring to her voice.

During her lunch hour, she had been out and purchased four cloth napkins. She unfolded one and laid it across my knees. Then she handed me another one.

"Have they been washed?" I asked.

She hesitated just a second before replying. "No, Mrs. Drodge, they have not been washed. They are a gift. I am not in the habit of washing gifts before I give them. They will have to do for now but I will take the other two home with me, wash them tonight and return them tomorrow. As part of the gift I will continue to do this for you as long as you are here."

"Thank you, Eleanor." I said. "Forgive me. That was very ungracious of me."

But the lesson wasn't over yet. She pulled up a chair and got straight to the point.

In short, I needed help, first with my attitude and then with my situation. She went on to explain that she understood my frustration. It seems her father had lost his sight five years previously through diabetes. He had experienced similar problems but now functions as a completely independent adult and still lives alone in his own home.

"Well good for him," I said.

Ignoring my petulance, she continued. "Help is available, you just need to ask and then be willing to accept it and work on the problem. I will help you if you wish but you must take the initiative." She stood up. "I'll leave you to think about it."

I admit that I am, in part, responsible for my own demise. Only in part, mind you. You see, I discovered love one day quite unexpectedly. I was a second year commerce student at Trinity College in Dublin. Initially, the relationship was tied up with sex—yes, crazy, free, wonderful sex. My dear! You'd be surprised at the goings on, I was surprised! I was known to be haughty, even a bit of a prude — look but don't dare touch! I was often referred to by those who envied me as "Her Ladyship." Usually when I made an appearance, some local yokel hunched over his pint would do a half-turn over his shoulder and mutter just loud enough for me to hear, "Gangway, lads, here comes Her Ladyship."

One day, I happened to mention to a school friend, Lydia Johnston, that I was having a wonderful fling with a medical student I had met. She was dumbfounded. "What, I don't believe it! A nobody?"

Well, she didn't have to believe it. I relished the idea of being able to shock Miss Johnston and anyone else who wanted to jump on that bandwagon of disguised envy and veiled whispers. When it came to justifying my wild romps in Dublin I thought of Granny and her secret smile and placed her on my side. Not that she would have openly approved, but I persuaded myself that she would understand and placed in my position may even have done the same herself. Granny still whispers to me from time to time. Even from the grave she strives for control. But I stopped listening years ago.

My father referred to Granny, his mother-in-law, as "The Duchess." She, in turn, referred to him as "that man." They annoyed each other intensely. My father, Edward Carter, brought wealth to the marriage. "New money," Granny would sniff, looking about as if a bad odor had penetrated the area. Daddy's great-grandmother had made a fortune working from a donkey and cart collecting betting money from the well-to-do, to be placed on the horses at the local betting shop. It seems she made most of her money fiddling the bets. She ended up owning a string of betting shops. That was where the real money came from. All this was part of ancient history, ancient enough to be conveniently forgotten.

The Bolfes, on the other hand, brought position and status. Granny liked to tell how, as a debutante, she had been presented at the court of King Edward VII. She'd say, "I was quite the beauty, you know. My dress came from Paris, of course." Then she'd describe the frothy cloud of white silk tulle, all ribbons and bows, and her pearls, her exquisite pearls with diamond clasp — a family heirloom.

This was followed by a little demure simpering. "I caused quite a stir at the palace. Even the king commented, although his words I found to be disagreeable. 'Ah,' he announced, loud enough to be heard all around, 'so this is the beauty from Connaught.' Connaught had the distinction of being the most backward part of rural Ireland. I was miffed but I curtsied deeply, gave him my most brilliant smile and called him a buffoon under my breath. I was in demand, my dance card was full to capacity and that was what mattered."

That secret smile of hers would settle at the corners of her mouth, which always left with me the impression that Granny could be naughty if she so chose.

When the Irish Republicans took over, it was the end of everything. The Bolfes were turned out of the grand estate that they had held for hundreds of years. Their house and its treasures was looted and burned to the ground. It made no difference that, according to Granny, she personally was a bit of a Republican sympathizer and had, on one occasion, given shelter to the famous rebel, Sean McBride. He in return had given her his spyglass as a token of his esteem. It was Granny's view that the Bolfes were good landlords who always saved the scraps from the kitchen for the poor and dispossessed, but despite all that, in her eyes, the Bolfes were now nothing more than the leftovers from a previous era.

I too feel like a leftover now. Around me I smell decay, the wilting, withering, wretched scraps of the life I am left with. Luckily, I still have my wits about me. There's no one in this place with whom I can have a decent conversation. They're all gaga. Seeing them makes me even more determined to hold on to my wits. That's why I am talking to you. You see I have an excellent memory and, as my sight fails, my memory seems to become more acute.

Perhaps I am more focused because I have to be. A little imagination also goes a long way.

Today is Friday. The weekend is at hand. These days they say T.G.I.F. with great enthusiasm — "Thank God it's Friday" — as if it matters. What damn difference does it make? Every day brings the same: breakfast, wash, dress, lunch, dinner, bed. The one good thing about Friday is that Eleanor comes on duty.

There was a letter today from Claire. Claire is my daughter but one would never know. She has a brilliant mind but is as dowdy as a pea hen, not even a stain of lipstick to brighten her up. She looks like her father's side of the family. You'd never believe that she is thirty-seven years old and a highly qualified medical doctor. She spends her life flitting around the world tending to the needs of the underprivileged. "Very rewarding," she tells me. Good God.

Apparently she fancies herself a latter day Norman Bethume. Then again, what can one expect from the kind of woman who chooses to pitch her tent in the jungles of Africa or the deserts of Outer Mongolia? Ridiculous nonsense. She writes to me about the strange goings-on in these backward places. I trust only Eleanor to read the letters to me.

In today's letter, Claire writes:

> This week I am attending patients in a town several miles from the hospital. It is really only a large clearing dotted with a few dozen, small, family huts and a colourful market that sells everything from nails to bales of fabric — their Walmart. My alarm clock here is the clang of cooking utensils in the quiet of dawn. The women are up and about very early. All chores are done outdoors, cooking, eating, washing, cleaning, socializing. I have a woman who comes and does all this for me. I should never manage otherwise. In the evening after work I love to sit outside and watch the colourful palette of people amble by, their laughter and banter echoing through the town. The children run

*around half-naked playing simple games with sticks and stones
or bits of rubbish. They are happy little souls, plagued by all
manner of deformities sometimes only visible to the trained eye.
I am here to help but many are beyond help.*

*Last night there was a festival of some kind. The men appeared
out of the darkness carrying flaming torches. They began to sing,
a slow rhythmic beat to begin, feet pounding the dry earth, the
tempo rising. It felt slightly eerie at first as if something sinister
was about to happen, but as the pace quickened and the voices
rose in unison the atmosphere grew triumphant and happy.
It went on well into the night.*

*Every night a different kind of concert happens; the frogs
perform. Yes, frogs. As darkness falls a chorus of croaking frogs
takes the stage. The noise is deafening and lasts about a half-
hour and then as if on cue from the baton of a conductor, the
concert abruptly ends.*

*Next time I write, Mother, I will tell you about Fatu Samba,
a young woman who has been thrown out of her home by her
husband because of an infected fistula but with surgery and a
little help has turned her life around and is training to be my
assistant.*

*Your daughter,
Claire*

Eleanor and I agree that this all makes for wonderful reading. If only
it was fiction. I cannot understand how Claire has chosen this lifestyle.
Then again, maybe I should try. After all, like me, she has made her
choices.

Jack Drodge was my choice. He came into my life one evening in the
spring of 1958, at a party in Dublin where we were both at university. He
was a medical student. I was not in the habit of paying attention to the
ordinary types who stood around drinking beer all night, completely
ignoring the women until it was near time for home, when, with bleary
eyes, they'd begin scanning the room looking for a likely one who might

be interested in "a little ride." Oh! How I loathed that type — Dublin fellows for the most part, who played rugby and at the end of the day, thought themselves entitled to a reward for their exertions on the field.

Jack came to my attention for one reason and one reason only. Unlike most of the Irish men of my acquaintance, he was agreeably tall. When you're five foot ten inches and a woman, being able to look up at a man and at the same time wear a pair of high-heel shoes is a bonus. He was a plain looking fellow with a broad, heavy-set face and a nose too long and tending to be slightly bulbous — the kind of nose that could become quite unsightly in years to come. He had good posture, however, and well-polished, leather shoes; a knife-edge crease in his flannels gave him a well-heeled look, making him very presentable by most standards. A wing of straight, fairish hair hanging loosely over one eye imparted a kind of dash he could never have otherwise achieved. He appeared to be quite spirited, quick to laughter but otherwise, I thought, unremarkable.

As the evening wore on, a chair across from me became available. Suddenly he was standing there smiling broadly, looking down on me as if we had known each other all our lives. Without asking my permission, he sat down.

"Your hair is magnificent," he said as if continuing a conversation already in progress.

I was used to receiving compliments on my luxurious titian hair so I acknowledged the tired compliment with a slow condescending smile. Then he surprised me.

"You put me in mind of the pirate queen, Grace O'Malley."

"And what would you know about Grace O'Malley?"

"And why shouldn't I know about Grace O'Malley?"

"You're a Canadian."

"Ah, you've been asking about me then." He grinned affably and thrust out his big hand. "Jack Drodge," he said. "From St John's, Newfoundland, and I do know a bit about Grace O'Malley." His eyebrows moved almost imperceptibly but enough to show that he objected to my questioning his knowledge.

I held his eyes but ignored his hand. "If you intend for the comparison to be a compliment," I said, "then you are mistaken. She was a harridan."

"Or a very striking and remarkable woman, depending on your point of view." The eyebrow moved again.

The deep resonance in his voice was beginning to lull me into complacency. "Enough!" Heads turned. I had raised my voice a shade too much to be acceptable so I stubbed out my cigarette and reached for my handbag, dropped my lighter and cigarettes inside, snapped the metal clasp shut, and stood to deliver my final shot. "Did you also know, Mr. Drodge, that this so-called striking and remarkable woman was purported to have been bald?"

Jack loved to recount this story verbatim to his friends, mimicking my hauteur as he spoke. I quite enjoyed reliving the exchange, although he always told it to amuse others.

Later, on reflection, I regretted my rudeness. After all, he had been polite, even amusing, so why did I have to dismiss him like that? No wonder I had the reputation for being haughty. I was haughty. I am haughty, and I am not ashamed to say that I still shun the common touch. I know that I am sometimes referred to here as "the bitch." I loathe such common language; I believe it is just a refuge for those who can do no better. But, I will admit to you, sometimes I envy the freedom that comes these days with just letting go, lashing out verbally at whatever or whoever clutters the space.

Perhaps, one of these days, now that I am conveniently out of earshot, I might practice using some choice words. For instance, that girl this morning — suppose I'd shot back, "Oh, bugger off!" or, "Go to hell! BUGGER OFF, YOU SILLY GIRL!"

Oh, dear, no, it catches in my throat. Maybe not. Well, I'll see.

Some of the younger staff have so little professional pride, they come through here with their mouths stuffed full of bubble gum. Common girls, they remind me of the sort my son James used to associate with: fleshy bosomed types, bulging like tavern wenches, jaws chewing on a knob of gum like a cow at the cud. Seeing that pink slippery knob appear every so often reminded one of a bulging third eye rolling around in a wet fleshy socket. This carry-on usually reached its peak when the pale, milky membrane of a bubble appeared and then CRACK, it was gone and the practice began all over again.

I must admit that the woman James married is clever and from a suitable family — but then, to have snapped up a well-educated man like James, one would need to be clever. James is, or rather was — I am not sure these days — a chartered accountant and was charming, full of life and energy like his father but, well... I'm glad his father is not around to witness the rest of this story.

Here comes the tepid-tea trolley. Why is it so difficult in an establishment like this to produce a decent cup of tea with a biscuit served on a plate instead of in a plastic bag? Is it so much to ask?

Now, where was I before I got sidetracked? Yes, venting my frustrations. I believe it has perked me up!

Fred, a friend of Jack's who lived in our basement for many years, had a facility for coarse language. He used it mostly when the men were gabbing and drinking together. He could certainly hold his own. If only I'd had him coach me, I'd be an expert now!

He was a ferrety kind of creature; slight with dark, glittery eyes that peered out from under big, heavy, black eyebrows. He wore circular, wire framed eyeglasses which, when removed, revealed two circles a shade or two lighter than the rest of his face and gave him that distinct look of a ferret. To cap it all, his clothes were frequently a size too big, which made him look even more diminutive and comical. When I first met him I wanted to laugh outright when this strange little fellow was introduced to me as Jack's buddy, Fred. I could hardly believe my eyes.

I could never fathom that relationship; Jack, a well-dressed, well-educated professional man and Fred, a minor shopkeeper's son who appeared to have no job and no purpose in life. The family lived above the shop but moved away when the business failed. Fred opted to stay behind in St John's and the Drodge family eventually took him in. Jack was studying in Ireland at the time.

I asked Jack about this odd arrangement one day.

"Fred and I are like brothers. Growing up we practically lived together — we did our homework together, played together and he usually stayed for dinner," Jack explained. "Sometimes he'd sleep over. I was an only child so my parents were delighted to have another child around."

He said all this as if it was the most natural thing in the world. Well, maybe to him, but not to me. Little wonder his parents' house was so chaotic — a haunt for every oddball who passed by, or so it seemed to me. I could hardly bear to step inside the door.

Jack's family owned a fair-sized house on Queen's Road overlooking the harbour. This became our house when they died. Queen's Road runs into New Gower Street, so the boys basically lived at opposite ends of the same street but a respectable distance apart. When I first met Fred, he told me how Jack and he had gone to school together. "In the same class," he said, with some pride.

"You mean the same grade." I said. He either missed the inference or simply chose to ignore me. I fancy now, it was the latter.

When we moved into the house on Queen's Road, Fred was already ensconced in the basement. "I cannot have *him* living in my house. It's like having a lodger or a street person living with us," I told Jack.

"Fred is having a hard time right now. He needs help and I must help him."

To me the whole arrangement was an embarrassment and caused an ongoing problem for Jack and me. But Jack would not have it otherwise.

I'm not sure that "lived" is the correct word to use for Fred's position in our household. Holed-up would better describe the situation. He had a room. He ate elsewhere, although if there were leftovers Jack would take them down to Fred. "You are just encouraging him," I'd say and Jack would shrug.

Fred used my laundry room to wash, which was way too personal for my liking but when Jack gave him permission to do his laundry in my washing machine that was more than I could handle.

"He can't do that," I said.

"Why not?"

"Because I don't want his damn underwear hanging in my laundry facility. I don't wish to share my personal space with him. Is that so hard to understand? There are public facilities available for people like him."

"He's not a stranger, but I'll speak to him about the underwear."

And so it continued — constant disagreements over Fred.

What could I do? It wasn't my house. It was willed to Jack. Eventually I became accustomed to the comings and goings downstairs. He hung around when Jack was about and sometimes they played chess together or headed off to a hockey game or out to the pub down the street in the evening. Fred usually left the house around noon every day and returned when he knew Jack was home from work. I never knew where he went or what he did. Nor did I care, but I never forgave Jack for disregarding my wishes and willfully putting our lives together in jeopardy. You see for ten years after we married it was just Jack and me. There were no children yet, so when we inherited his parents' house, Fred was like an ever-present, suffocating shadow on our relationship.

Class was very important to me then. I thought myself sophisticated, entitled to whatever it was that I wanted. I expected to be treated differently. To have people do my bidding. Growing up, I observed within our immediate circle how people bullied their way to positions of power, took what they wanted. The lower orders were there to serve. I knew nothing of the real world or its ways, nor did I want to. My first real foray outside of my own circle was when I went away to university and met Jack. I was an innocent abroad.

The summer following our first encounter, I heard that Jack Drodge had gone back to Newfoundland for the holidays and as usual I went to Kilgraney, our stud farm. Since childhood I had been a member of the Kildare Pony Club and had spent most of my free time riding and training for Three Day Eventing. This was tough competition, demanding hard work and intensive training. It was made up of dressage on Day 1, cross country on Day 2, and show jumping on Day 3. The plan to get a better horse had worked perfectly and I now rode a beautiful Irish sport horse called Saoirse. The name means *freedom* in the Irish language. It was not my choice but it suited her perfectly. We made a handsome pair, matched in every way even to our hair colour. We were also fierce competitors.

The summer after I met Jack, I was chosen to compete at a major event in England. I was the youngest member of the team but did exceptionally well and got a real taste of tough competition and I loved it. Early in the afternoon of the third day we were relaxing after an exceptional round. Excitement was mounting as we realized that winning was within our grasp. Then disaster struck. A horse from another team kicked Saoirse hard on her right front leg and in that instant, everything changed. I saw the bulging terror in her eyes, heard father yelling for a vet and then silence.

I shut out everything around me except for Saoirse. My grip tightened on her halter. I drew her closer. We were a team again speaking our own special language — the language of togetherness, of finding spiritual union. I felt the shudder in her shoulders, heard the high-pitched whimper as the vet's big, gentle hands probed the tender area. I lay my head on her pulsing neck and knew in that instant that I had never loved another creature like I loved Saoirse. She was my partner — the other half of my life.

When eventually we retired to the stables and made her comfortable, the vet took me aside. I knew without hearing the words that our days of competing together as a team were over. I needed to be alone with my horse.

On weekends, I continued to ride to hounds with my father and went to all the social events. That lifestyle appealed to me, but only until it began to take on a different and more serious side. Daddy had plans and they were nearing fruition. He decided that with my knowledge and expertise with horses I should take over the stud farm with a view to expanding the business. I got ready to return to Dublin and finish my commerce degree at Trinity College, which would qualify me to handle the business side of the venture. It seemed a reasonable arrangement at the time but I wasn't wild about the idea.

It had been an exciting but heartbreaking summer and, back in Dublin, I was glad to have a plan. I didn't give any serious thought to the Canadian. Just the same, I was quietly keeping an eye out for him. When I walked into the Bective Rugby Club one evening early in the term, I spotted him right away. Head and shoulders above the crowd and deep in conversation with a group of friends. I remember feeling a rush of excitement.

However, rather than appear too keen, I began to move off in the opposite direction looking for my friend. I didn't get very far. A tap on the shoulder and there he was, looking fit and tanned, his hair lighter and even longer than before.

"I'm back," he said.

"So it would appear."

"Had a good summer?"

"Yes, I did, thank you. Now, if you'll excuse me," I said, "I'm looking for a friend." As I began to move away, he placed his hand under my elbow.

"She's over there. She's looking for you. Come with me."

"I don't need an escort," I said, shrugging him off.

"But you do need a drink. Gin and tonic, a tall glass, I believe, with a twist of lemon?"

Such tenacity! He was like a drone in the height of summer, constantly airborne and on alert, but in the end his persistence paid off. Something about Jack Drodge conjured up in me a kind of unbridled freedom, a euphoria which I welcomed and found to be unbearably exciting, but at times left me feeling trapped in that uncertain space between bewilderment and pure contentment. Never had I met anyone quite like Jack. He carried himself tall and erect with an assurance and panache that belied the reality. He was kind, considerate, fun loving and very attentive, which I found to be refreshing. He behaved in a gentlemanly, almost formal fashion, particularly in his dealings with women — no rutting and fumbling, no snapping of elastic. When morning came, despite my protests, he usually refused to linger. He was up early and gone to classes looking impeccable. This stubbornness infuriated me, but at the same time, intrigued me. He lured me to his bed with an ease and skill that could only have come with practice. Like a conjuror at the top of his game he mesmerized me and left me confused and captivated, wondering what on earth had come over me. It was his custom to undress slowly, placing his clothes neatly and precisely on the back of a chair, shoes tucked underneath, socks carefully pulled right-side out and placed on top.

This was something he continued to do all his life. In that way he was always ready to make love or answer a house call in the middle of the night and so would show up looking every bit the attending physician. But once the external persona was removed, formality ended there. He went about the task with the skill of a surgeon, exposing the layers of my virgin self until the very nub of my pride lay wide open, bare and pristine. He made love with wild and fierce abandon, and to my great surprise and delight, I found myself to be not only willing, but his equal. Night after night we gave our passion free rein, stopping from time to time to enjoy a cigarette. This was the only time he smoked. I felt no shame, no anxiety or loss, just wonder and pleasure, like I was receiving the perfect gift.

Oh, it was heavenly in that little third-storey flat looking out over the rooftops of Dublin. In the quiet of my morning I liked to linger, burying myself again in the warmth and comfort of the bed to savour the memory, wondering, with every tick of the clock by my bedside, if I was losing my mind. I made excuses for my indolence: I needed time on my own to think. The lecture that morning was not important and I was tired, so I lay on, curled in the hollow womb of our lovemaking, and dreamed of what the future might hold.

I was twenty years old then and, as you can imagine, I had begun to conjure up a romantic, exciting life for Jack and me. It had to do with a large, well-appointed house reflecting my style and discriminating taste, where Jack and I could host splendid dinner parties and social gatherings within the Canadian expat community. My head was filled with images of salmon fishing expeditions to remote fishing lodges in wild, uninhabited territories and shooting parties on the open tundra for birds, caribou, deer, even bears. Jack had described to me ice skating on frosty winter nights across frozen ponds, a big fire burning brightly on the ice, and hot mulled wine followed by dinner at a friend's country home just outside St. John's. I had seen pictures of the rugged beauty of Canada and the images were etched in living colour in my imagination. Kilgraney Stud Farm, with all the trappings of horse-country life, seemed tame and stuffy by comparison and with my competing life at a standstill, the idea of Canada was made even more interesting. But as the morning dragged on and the sheets cooled in my love nest, so too did my ardour and then, like the aftermath of a bad dream, uncertainty began to throb in my veins. Kilgraney, the horses, the comforts, my position, all the things that I had come to expect from life were mine for the taking. My only brother, Edward, obsessed with the poetry of John Donne, had departed the fold to bury himself in the libraries of Oxford University. He had made it quite clear that "cleaning up after thoroughbreds" for the rest of his life was not on his agenda. So the thought of leaving everything behind and heading off into the unknown with a man I had met just a few months previously was a decision not to be taken lightly.

My parents, of course, were another matter but, I persuaded myself, with Jack's encouragement, it was my life and my decision. As the weeks passed, the notion of Kilgraney Stud Farm becoming my life's work seemed less and less attractive.

By the end of term I had made up my mind. I was going to marry Jack Drodge and move to Canada. I rather relished the idea of sharing the news that I was breaking free, off on an adventure!

I look back now and wonder, if I had been less vulnerable and better prepared for what was ahead, would things have worked out differently? I had no idea of the reality of small-town life in a harsh climate, but I was so wrapped up in my newfound freedom that I ignored the signs and started thinking about my trousseau and planning the wedding.

The invitation for Jack and I to spend the holidays with my family arrived a few days before Christmas. I was anxious that everything should go smoothly so I suggested that Jack have his hair trimmed for the occasion, but the idea was dismissed summarily. However, aware of my apprehension, he showed up on the day of our departure with an exquisite bouquet of fresh flowers for my mother.

"She'll like that," I said. "She likes attention."

It was midday on Christmas Eve when we set out in my little green Triumph Spitfire for Kilgraney. It was an unusual day. Overnight, a heavy hoar frost had covered the land with a spectacular veil of glitter. The pastures, the bare trees, the paddocks and barns and the hawthorn hedges looked particularly festive and beautiful. Hard ruts in the laneways were covered with a light dusting of snow. The roads were slick and treacherous, the driving difficult. I was as nervous as a two-year-old filly at the starting gate. Jack on the other hand was relaxed and happy, noting every detail of the countryside.

When we turned off the road and in through the big iron gates I announced proudly, "This is Kilgraney."

He turned to me. "You never say home. You never call it home."

"The house has a name. Just like you. It is a special house, Georgian and…"

He was paying no attention. When I pulled up outside the house he was out of the car, standing on the gravel driveway surveying the property before I had even turned the engine off.

He didn't acknowledge me when I joined him but continued to focus on the house, remarking on the faded pinkish hue of the old brick and the spidery network of winter-bare vines climbing the walls.

"Cool and green in the summer, warm and red in the fall. Lovely." He seemed a trifle wistful.

"You're right. It's a beautiful house." I tucked into his side looking for warmth.

He pointed to the symmetrical placement of the small-paned sash windows, how they reached almost to the ground. He admired the startling white painted trim and the architectural detail on the glossy black front door and portico.

I had expected him to be impressed with the beauty and charm of the old house, but I was surprised by his keen interest in the architecture. Suddenly, I saw us both as if from a faraway place; a couple of strangers who had unexpectedly come face to face in a clearing. The look on their faces is one of alarm — or is it wonder? At that moment he turned and quietly scanned my face.

"What is it, Jack?"

"I was just thinking how lovely you look here in your own surroundings."

I had taken care with how I dressed for the occasion; the lavender cashmere twin-set Mummy had given me for my birthday and Granny Bolfe's pearls, always appropriate and very dear to me. The slim tweed skirt that came just below my knees was chosen for him. Jack, noticing a shiver pass through me, reached into the car for my coat and put it over my shoulders. He dipped back again for the bouquet of flowers.

"Anyone home do you think?"

As if on demand the front door opened and my father stepped into the picture. He raised his hand, giving us the royal wave, or was it an off-hand salute? I couldn't decide. I took Jack's arm and walked towards the door. The crunch of gravel beneath our feet filled the dead space in between. I kissed Father's cheek then turned to introduce Jack.

"Glad to meet you, sir." Jack offered his hand.

"Welcome to Kilgraney. Your mother is waiting in the drawing-room."

At Christmastime I often think about the close comfort of the house; it looked so wonderful at that time of year: the tree standing in the corner glittering with lights and beautifully decorated, the winter smell of pine vaguely present in the house, the wood fire warm and inviting. On that particular Christmas Eve, Mummy, her white hair swept into a soft wave on top of her head, sat in her usual spot in the sitting room to the left of the fireplace. She was dressed from head to toe in dove-grey with two strings of large, equally sized pearls at her throat. Surrounded by the cozy depth of over-stuffed chintz and the rich permanence of the Persian rug, she looked poised and elegant. By her side, her beloved spaniel, Charlie, lay recumbent. His head came up as I entered the room. Well-behaved, as was expected, Charlie rose to his feet and came to greet me, lowering his head to have his silky ears scratched. He then dutifully returned to his former position.

My grand piano, a gift rarely opened and still gleaming with newness, stood in the corner, a silver bowl full of red-berried holly artfully placed on top. The piano had arrived on my sixteenth birthday to replace an old one that had been in the family for years. It came with a trunk load of demands and expectations, enough to turn a true pleasure into an irksome chore. So it sat there unused and unloved.

"Darling." Mummy suddenly came to life and offered her delicate cheek to be kissed. "You look charming in lavender." She smelled vaguely of Dior, detected only by those who got close enough. When Jack stepped up and presented her with the flowers, she nodded appreciatively; friendly but formal. Her eyes swept over him registering neither approval nor disapproval — a good sign. Talk was polite and pleasant as we discussed the road conditions on the way down.

"Is Edward coming for Christmas?" I asked.

"No, I understand he has other commitments." Mummy looked away.

When Jack accepted the offer of a drink, he was given a whiskey and soda, which, thankfully, he accepted without question although I knew rum would be more to his liking. Mummy and I had sherry.

Later, dinner was served in the dining room. It was a hearty and delicious procession of steaming carrot and ginger soup, crown of pork decked out with white frillies, crunchy roast potatoes and stuffed baked apples bursting from their glossy golden jackets. This perked me up; we hadn't eaten since breakfast and Jack was hungry. The wine was excellent and of a good vintage. So, feeling relaxed and very replete, Jack ventured into the world of Irish politics about which he considered himself to be somewhat conversant and which he naturally thought was a safe enough bet, knowing that Daddy, besides being a barrister, held a seat in the Senate. Things were going nicely until the subject switched to Canada and Newfoundland, about which, I was sure, my parents knew little or nothing.

"I believe there is good fishing off the coast," my father said in an off-hand kind of way.

"Cod. Cod fish," Mummy chirped. "The colony…" Her voice cracked and she coughed daintily behind her thin hand. When we all turned to look in her direction she clamped up and cast an eye around as if looking to see who had spoken.

"You are right, Mrs. Bolfe-Carter," Jack said politely. "The industry —"

Daddy interrupted with a question. "Am I correct in saying that Newfoundland is no longer a British possession?"

We all turned to look in his direction. My jaw began to ache. I knew what he was up to. He was carefully guiding the witness. Jack answered politely, giving a brief summary of how Newfoundland became a province of Canada in 1949. Daddy listened attentively. I noticed his moustache twitch; he was smiling. His mustache hid his teeth. They were long and crooked. I knew this because he had surgery on his mouth one time and the mustache had to go. My father was a handsome man, but without the mustache he looked a fright!

"I see," he said, fingering his mustache, and immediately suggested we retire to the drawing room. He had completed his preliminary round of cross-examination.

Cigars were offered and Jack declined. Daddy took his position in front of the fire and began to trim and roll his cigar. He looked at Jack quizzically, taking his measure. He was back in cross-examination mode, biding his time, probing for the weak spot in his opponent. Slice and dice, he used to call it when referring to his technique as a barrister at law.

"Drodge. That is an unusual name," he said, rocking back and forth, heel to toe, the shiny black toe caps of his shoes appearing and disappearing like a couple of wet rodents scuttling for cover.

"There are a few of us around."

"Jack is one of us." I interjected hastily. "Not Roman Catholic," I added for Jack's information. Father ignored me.

"Your father is a businessman, I understand?"

"Yes, he is." Jack seemed delighted to switch to a new topic. "The business has been in the family now for three generations." He sipped his whiskey and began to relate the story of how the building of the first railway across Newfoundland and a timely marriage had brought major contracts to the small company and insured its success when the next question came, quick, straight and sharp as an arrow — and just as deadly.

"And what is the nature of the business?"

"Plumbing. Plumbing supplies and —"

"Plumbing!" Daddy was taken off guard. Like a string puppet he sprang into action: his head twitching and turning, his arms rising and falling in short, jerky motions as if someone was tugging the strings.

There was a sharp intake of breath from Mummy before she looked away.

The reaction was not lost on Jack, but he continued, seemingly unperturbed. I tried to suppress a giggle which in actual fact was panic.

Mummy gave me a harsh look. Inappropriate laughter had always been a problem for me.

"Yes, my great-grandfather's sister Dorothy married into the Reid family, who built the railway across Newfoundland. My family secured major contracts to supply materials for this venture which, as you can imagine, was very lucrative." Jack raised his glass in a kind of salute. "The rest as they say —"

There was a hint of jocularity in his voice so at that point I jumped in. "Jack is studying to be a medical doctor. He hopes to become a consultant in internal medicine."

Jack laughed. "The joke in the family is that I am to be a different kind of plumber. I should by rights study urology and get down to the real business of bodily function."

Mummy looked up. Her small mouth formed a perfect O but no sound came out.

Jack's glass was now empty and with a mischievous chuckle, he eyed the glass and said, "Our family theme song is 'Danny Boy.' You know, the pipes the pipes are caw..aw..ling." Now Jack intoned the line in his rather fine baritone voice, puffing out his chest with mock pride. Panic hit again, a tight fist squeezing tighter. He was all set to give the full rendition when Mummy exclaimed, "Oh dear!" and began to pat her chest fretfully, making a pretense at coughing.

Jack's glass was still empty so I rushed over to Mummy's side.

"Jack," I managed to get out, "can play the piano and he likes to sing. Do play for us Jack and we can sing some carols. After all it is Christmas Eve. Mummy would love that. Wouldn't you, Mummy?"

"Maybe you can play for us, darling. One of those examination pieces that you knew so well. The music is still there in the piano stool. It has been so long since I've heard you play and you have such an exquisite touch." She smiled at me like I was her little puppet.

I shook my head. "Perhaps another time, Mummy. I'm out of practice now."

"You play the piano, Sylvia? I didn't know." Jack looked from one to the other of us for confirmation.

"Yes, she has all her certificates from the Royal Conservatory."

Mummy was prepared to continue but I gave Jack an urgent look that said, "Hush!" and proceeded to lead him to the piano in the corner. I placed a chair for Mummy beside him. Daddy chose to stand apart from the group, his arms folded across his chest. Jack struck a chord and we were off. He sang to Mummy, coaxing her to join in by playing softly while lowering his own voice. Mummy smiled shyly at Jack and began to warble, a line here and there in her high-pitched birdie voice and then she took off on her own.

> I dreamt I lived in marble halls
> With vassals and serfs by my side,
> And of all that assembled within these walls
> That I was the hope and the pride.
> I had riches all too great to count,
> Could boast of a high ancestral name,
> But I also dreamt which pleased me most…

At that point Daddy walked out of the room and her voice faded in his wake.

The evening ended with… *goodwill henceforth to earth and men begin and never cease…* la de da de da. Mummy continued to sing for several bars after the last notes had sounded. Like a little sparrow she was trying to be heard until she realized that no one was listening, then she stopped abruptly. Everything was suddenly silent, unnaturally silent, like nobody knew what to say.

I said, "Merry Christmas."

What a strange evening that was. As the lid came down on the piano, I knew that despite his apparent good humour, Jack would no longer consider asking my father for my hand in marriage. He had read the situation perfectly. He was not a suitable match for Edward Carter's only daughter. I could tell he was furious but outwardly he looked unperturbed. He was not about to plead with me or for me.

"It is your decision, Sylvia," he said later. "You must decide."

That was his final word on the subject. He then went about the business of studying in earnest for his final exams. I am not sure if Jack had second thoughts then, but if he did, he never said and I never asked.

The final confrontation with my father came later on, in the spring when I went on my own to Kilgraney to tell my parents of my decision. My mother took her usual position in her chair by the fire; my father took his in front of the fire and Charlie came to have his ears rubbed. There were yellow daffodils in a deep blue vase on the piano. The picture perfect scene could have been from a film. It lasted no more than ten minutes.

"Love, my arse," My father bellowed. His common background always showed when he was angry. "All you care about now is jumping into bed with that plumber fellow. Money is what counts, money and position. Out there in the backwoods, you'll have neither. You mark my words. You'll be high-tailing it back here within a few years, divorce in hand with your brats in tow. Well my girl, in this country they will be regarded as bastards."

I turned to my mother for support, but she just flapped her hands like a grounded petrel and looked away.

"That, Father, is insulting." I was trying hard to sound spirited. "I want neither your money, your chattels, nor your acquired position. I am here simply as a courtesy to you and Mummy."

I left then and went to the barn to say good-bye to Saoirse. I told her that in time I would send for her and we'd be together again. I collected my clothes from my bedroom, threw them in the back of the car and drove away. That was the last time I stood in our house. The last time I saw Saoirse. Later, I had a sneaking feeling that I had been rash, that there was some truth in what Father had to say, but his final insult put an end to my concerns and fuelled my resolve. It made me more determined than ever to go my own way and prove him wrong. I had always been a risk taker but when I met Jack a kind of madness came over me and so I blundered on.

When Jack finished his medical degree that spring we went to England and were married in a registry office on Paddington Road in London. Just like that, Sylvia Bolfe-Carter became plain old Sylvia Drodge.

My son, James, asked me once why we never went to Ireland to visit our grandparents and when I told him why, he looked at me aghast and said, "Big mistake, Mother. You just didn't deal with your father correctly. You could have had it all."

I let it go, but later, I wondered if he demonstrated spunk or if I had a wily young fox on my hands. He was twelve years old then and Jack was still alive.

My eyes get worse by the day. It is like seeing through tears; everything is a blur.

To complicate matters I tripped on a corner of the rug, fell over and broke my hip and that is what has landed me in this place; this home for the aged and infirm: "for rehabilitation and my own protection" — so they tell me. I did have home help but the medical people insist that they know what is best for me. With a broken hip, doing the simplest things, like washing and dressing, is more difficult. They tell me that had I left the stove on and unattended, that I could have burned the house down. I am constantly bombarded with advice, none of which I have asked for or want. Living here is just a temporary solution until I can get around on my own.

I just want to go home to my own house where I can be independent and have my own things but I have so little fight left in me. Eleanor tells me there is help available at the C.N.I.B. — the Canadian Institute for the *Blind*, for heaven's sake! — but I cannot even think about this. Eleanor says she is willing to take me there or have an advisor come to visit me. I cannot bear the thought of tapping along Gower Street with a white cane. I won't do it! It is absolutely out of the question!

I have nothing left but memories: memories of our torrid and wonderful love affair, memories of those years when we were first married, when I was willing to ignore the hardship of the life, when I chose to hope for a better day when I could have the comfortable, romantic life I dreamed of. Those lean years when his parents kept us solvent; paid for our first house — a tiny bungalow — another one of their many handouts. It was an embarrassment.

One day a piano arrived at the door. The delivery man insisted it was for us. I called Jack at the office.

"There's a piano being delivered," I said.

"It's a gift from Dad. You can play now, Sylvia. You'll enjoy that."

"I don't want another damn piano, Jack. If your father insists on giving us another handout, tell him your wife wants a dining-room table." I was seething. "Don't try to fool yourself, Jack, and don't try to fool me. That piano is for you and Fred and your friends to hammer out your jingles. It has nothing to do with what I want. Besides, who said I wanted to play the piano again?"

The whole town knew about the piano and where it came from. There are no secrets around here.

Two youngsters standing on the pavement were watching the whole charade — the piano half off the truck, two delivery men waiting, front door wide open and me in the hall on the phone, and I heard one say to the other, "Must be a big run on toilets these days!" He was making rude gestures as he spoke and the men were laughing.

Memories, they come and go like the tide, linger for a time and then begin to recede. Others come with the force and urgency of flood waters, their clarity and intensity often leaving me struggling for air, trembling with delight or rocked by anger and terror. Like that desperate afternoon when Jack collapsed.

We had been married for twenty years by then and had two children. Jack's parents had died and we had inherited their house and business. I had hopes for the future.

I was standing in the kitchen, a brace of partridge, pink fleshed and oven ready lying on the countertop. The dining table was set for two with white linen and candles. I had learned to cook out of necessity but had come to enjoy the process. Over time I had acquired some china and silverware and had learned to host some formal dinner parties and invite people in the town to dine with us. I liked to try new recipes so I bought a copy of *Mrs. Beaton.* So I was busy that day, happily working on the finer details of cooking partridge in red-wine sauce. It was to be a romantic evening, just Jack and me for dinner by the fireside.

The phone in the hallway disturbed my reverie. I hurried out hoping it was Jack, wiping my hands on my apron, fluffing my hair as if he could actually see me. I wanted to remind him about the special dinner, and to ask him to pick up a good Beaujolais.

"Hello," I said, bright and eager but the voice on the phone was strange and the tone precise. An urgent summons was worming its way down the line and into the hallway.

"Mrs. Drodge, we have your husband here," the voice said.

"Jack?"

"You need to come."

"Need?"

"Right away, Mrs. Drodge."

"Right away?"

The words continued to tumble down the line like a drum roll, a beat to action that prompted my body to move but my brain to freeze. I hung up, went back to the kitchen. What to do? I removed the apron and laid it on the table, went back to the hall, slipped on a jacket, rummaged in a drawer for a lipstick, ran it along my top and bottom lip and headed for the door. Max, Jack's dog, yelped. It was an urgent query. He tilted his head to one side, blocking my exit and waiting for an answer. I pushed him aside. The car must have known the way, for somehow, I arrived in a timely manner at the hospital and parked. I realized I did not ask a single question on the phone, or if I did, I didn't listen to the answers so I had no idea what had happened or why I was there.

There were questions, forms to be filled in, people all talking at once and then a waiting-room — a special waiting-room, empty and not for the general public. It said so on the door. There were green vinyl chairs along the walls and a telephone on a table in the corner. I picked a chair and sat down. I realized I was still in my slippers; silly, pink furry slippers. I whipped my feet under the chair, out of sight.

James had given the slippers to me for Christmas. He was away at school in Quebec. I thought that a little French polish and acquiring another language might be a good idea. Sending him to school in Europe was out of the question — too expensive. Quebec was the next best thing. I realized that I should phone him but I couldn't bring myself to get up and use the phone.

A young couple came in and sat across from me. The man was crying and the woman was cradling his head. I suddenly remembered Claire. Everything had slowed down. I couldn't recall where she was and then it came to me. She was at school — no, at a friend's home for a sleepover.

There was so much noise in the corridor. Banging and hammering. Two men in yellow hard hats came in. They stood in the middle of the room studying plans and drawings. The woman across the room was on the phone, her hand cupped around the receiver. The men began to stack and remove the green chairs. They nodded an apology in my direction. The chairs on my left went first, then the ones on the right. I was marooned, my back to the wall. The men came and went, oblivious to the real drama all around them.

A nurse with a chart appeared and asked me to follow her. I flapped across the room in my pink slippers and out into the confusion of the corridor and then into another room. I recognized the man in the white coat coming from around the large desk but I could not recall his name nor did it register when he told me.

"I want to see my husband."

The man fingered the black cord of the stethoscope around his neck. "Jack collapsed right here in the hospital," he said. He indicated that I take a seat.

"He shouldn't be here. It's Saturday."

"He came to check on one of his patients."

"On Saturday?"

"Sylvia," he said, "I'm afraid Jack's condition is very serious. He has suffered a brain aneurism and is on life support."

I am not exactly sure when reality hit me or when it was that I finally got to see my husband or indeed what time had elapsed, but all the talk and explanation in the world could never have prepared me for the sight of Jack, lying there stiff and pale against the hard white lines of the hospital sheets. Something was edging to a close, I could feel it, sliding resolutely along like a weighty elevator door, and there was nothing I could do to stop its progress. The machine by the bed was beeping, a blue line dancing across the screen. I stared, mesmerized, foolishly expecting the dark, black clot of blood that nestled at the base of his brain to show itself. I don't know why I expected this to happen, and when it didn't, I flew into a rage and wheeled on the little group of doctors and nurses standing behind me. "Get out," I yelled. "Get out of here, all of you. Get out!"

They scurried for the door like frightened children.

I stayed by him all through that night, playing in my mind the ebbing story of our lives, the harmony that was ours for twenty years, the joy of love and closeness that I had never dreamed possible. No shadow of bitterness or disappointment crossed my mind that night, no thought of hardship, nothing to mar the peace and intimacy of that space. I believed that he could hear me, that he knew I was there because if I placed my ear to his lips I could feel the occasional, quick intake of breath when I whispered something that only he would know. As I talked, I traced the dips and hollows of his broad face, the nap of day-old stubble rough against my fingertips, and I heard the faint strains of a tune he always hummed as he shaved. It was his own composition, a loose arrangement of notes that varied slightly from day to day depending on his mood. A stranger would give him his final shave without song or ceremony.

I explored the line and contour of his hair, remembering our first afternoon together in the little flat and me, excited, giggling like a young girl. I gently massaged his head, breathing in the musky, man smell of his scalp, pulling it deep inside me so I should never forget. I massaged the rough feet that had plodded the barrens with Max by his side, and I kissed the crooked middle toe on his left foot and kissed it again and again but there was no reaction and I knew in that moment that I had truly lost him. I lay down beside him, wrapped the covers around us, my cheek resting on his warm chest, listening, listening wide-eyed to the steady pulse of his heart as it resolutely marched towards eternity. I sobbed and sobbed some more until I was gasping and sucking in great mouthfuls of air. Finally, after a bout of violent shuddering, I was spent. I slept then, my head still burrowing into his warm, damp chest and no one came to disturb our peace.

When morning came I kissed Jack as I always did, got up and went out, quietly closing the door behind me. At the nursing station I asked to see the doctor in charge. I was still in my pink slippers and jacket; stripped of pride, beyond caring, raw to the point where it no longer hurt. I was emptied out. I can barely remember what transpired other than hearing a request that I consider donating Jack's organs. I ignored the suggestion. Talk and more talk, deep shock and words of sympathy all around and then I left to locate my children.

James came home from Quebec the following day looking quite the young man. He kissed me, French style, on both cheeks; the double Judas they call it in Ireland. He then stepped into the role of man of the house quite naturally. When he donned the dark suit, purchased specially for the funeral, he looked older than his years but remarkably like his father. He wore the suit well although it hung loosely on his lanky boyish frame giving him that slightly awkward look that a youth assumes when put in a man's clothing to do a man's job. Later on I found out that he had taken an active role in making decisions on many of the arrangements but I don't recall any of that. Claire, on the other hand, who had just turned thirteen, always shy and deeply attached to her father, went to her room and locked the door. I could hear her sobbing well into the night but she refused to unlock the door or come out. Jack's dog, Max, found a spot by the front door and lay down to wait.

People came and went, food appeared and filled the refrigerator, the telephone rang incessantly and I had conversations that were lost or scrambled in the churn of activity.

Finally when the peace of night settled on the house, I went upstairs to sit in the dark by the bedroom window. Clutching Jack's pillow in my arms, I watched the city gradually close down. A light mist was falling, making the rooftops glisten in the street light. They were an oddly comforting sight. They reminded me of our little third-floor flat in Dublin;

the rooftops in the morning light stretching for miles, the door closing quietly behind Jack as he headed off to classes while I snuggled back down into the warmth and comfort of our bed to dream my dreams. I buried my face in his pillow again and cried myself into a choking, fitful sleep.

Later on, when I woke stiff and shivering, I pulled on Jack's thick woolen dressing gown and went down to the kitchen to make tea and have a cigarette. Max was still by the door, waiting. He opened one eye as I came down the stairs, shifted his position slightly and went back to waiting. It was as if the space had emptied out; every sound seemed magnified, the click of the light switch, the water hitting the bottom of the kettle, the hum of the refrigerator. Jack's absence coursed through the house like a creeping mist. It had settled into the walls, changed the air.

When the kettle shrieked, I jumped. It was then I noticed the figure standing at the top of the basement stairs. It was Fred, dressed for the outdoors in his shabby black wool coat and ancient soft-brimmed hat. He appeared to have shrunk over the last twenty-four hours, his coat even bigger and longer on his small frame. This time he put me in mind of a hapless crow.

"You alright?" he asked.

"Yes."

I regarded him for some time awaiting an explanation for his appearance.

"I can't sleep, Sylvia," he said. "I think I'll go for a walk."

Fred came and went by the basement door, so I inclined my head in that direction.

He turned, headed back down the stairs and I heard him go out. Of course, I knew what was on Fred's mind. In his head, he was family. The outdoor garb was just a ploy, a way to find a seat at the kitchen table.

I suppose he had been around long enough to be considered as family, but not in any way that I could understand. The whole notion was foreign to me. He attended our parties and Jack always invited him at Christmas time. Sometimes he came; sometimes he would just disappear for a period of time and then show up days or weeks later. I never paid too much attention to him but he was always respectful of me although he knew I disapproved of his presence in the house.

I have to admit that he and Jack were great together, always the life of the party. When Fred wasn't there, the party was never quite so good. They both loved to sing. They knew all the pop songs, ballads, songs from the shows, arias, whatever came to mind they knew it all and Jack pounded away on the piano. Fred was known around town as having a particularly good tenor voice and often sang lead roles in the big musicals. When they were together like that, there was no denying how close they were. Jack wanted him around all the time, even at our dinner parties, but I drew the line there.

Fred came back around two o'clock in the morning. I was still in the kitchen. I could hear him coming up Queen's Road singing at the top of his voice. *Hello Dolly, well, hello Dolly. It's so nice to have you back where you beeelong.* I rushed to the front door and there he was, strolling along running a stick, clickety clack, along the iron railings. *"You're lookin' swell Dolly /I can tell Dolly* — Ah fuck Dolly!"

"Fred," I called out, just loud enough to be heard. "Get in here at once."

He turned, saw me, smiled benevolently and said, "Just singing Jack home."

"Get in the kitchen. You're a disgrace. You can be heard all over town." I wished that Jack had never brought him into the house.

I made coffee and he slurped down two cups without uttering a word and I smoked yet another cigarette, watching him carefully and wondering what was to be done with Fred. I was about ready to send him on his way when he reached up, removed his hat and laid it on the table. His straight black hair lay flat to his head. He pasted it down still more with his hand. When he looked up there was pure misery in his eyes.

"It's fuckin' hopeless. Isn't it?"

I balked at the language but held my tongue. "No, there is no hope."

We sat there on opposite sides of the long wooden table, each caught up in their own reverie, a wife and a friend, crushed and spent like the cigarette ends in the ashtray.

"We played together as children, over there —" He indicated the far end of the table. "Cars , Ludo, fuckin' Snakes and Ladders. When that could no longer keep us happy we began to spread our wings and make up games. I was full of ideas for building things from scratch and Jack was willing to help make them a reality.

"I remember one time I rigged up a design for a mini-tank using a match box, elastic bands and wooden spools, the kind used for sewing thread. We set about building a prototype. We cut notches in the wooden rims of the spools for traction and propelled them along the table using the rubber bands and matchsticks. After several tries and a few adjustments, they were scooting along the table! My mother had a box full of these empty spools by her sewing machine so before long we had a fleet of automated tanks ready for action. It was Russians vs. Yanks. Bloody murder, tanks advancing from both sides, shells exploding, blood, guts everywhere. Mayhem!

"Jack thought they were brilliant. I remember him thumping me on the back, telling me he didn't know anyone who could come up with an idea like this, design it and damn well make it work. We got carried away then and made plans to make a kit and sell it at school."

I had never before had a conversation like this with Fred, had never taken time to listen to what he had to say. Running his hand back and forth on the deal tabletop, he went on, pausing briefly from time to time to apologize for his language and then he was off again in a kind of monologue, barely stopping for a breath, telling mostly about their childhood escapades, how Jack had always encouraged him to develop his ideas.

Fred finished up by telling me how proud he was when Jack went away to become a doctor.

All this time, Jack was at the forefront of my mind. He made it all happen. He was the vehicle, the magnet. He stepped into a room, things fell into place. People came to him, chatted, shook his hand, delighted in his company. He was relaxed, without guile or posturing, so approachable. I don't know how he ever came from that crazy home and parents. Me, I just came with the package — an appendage, an ornament. Jack's wife, from away. But Fred and Jack, they had a lifetime of connection. They were part of the landscape, sturdy perennials that suited the environment and flourished as an integral part of it.

I turned to look at Fred and wondered if all the people who regularly came to our house would still want to see me. Did I want to see them?

Would I still be a part of their circle? Would I matter anymore? Would they matter anymore?

As if reading my mind, Fred said, "When he brought you home, I thought you were the loveliest thing to walk the earth. I used to study you from a distance, back straight as a rampike, head held high, elegant and poised, a touch haughty, surveying the room like a fine-feathered bird. I often wondered what you thought of this place and the crowd of us."

He gave a short laugh and with a surprisingly elegant index finger, touched the edge of the ashtray and began to push the cigarette ends around in the ash. "No red rings," he said, referring to my trademark, lipstick ringed cigarette. He continued to shift the ends around. "I'd do anything for that man."

"Even tolerate me?" I reached for another cigarette, aware that I had opened a door, just a crack.

"You're a fine woman, Sylvia, times a little frosty but no harm in you. It's just how you are." After a pause he said, "The crowd around here isn't easy. They're not big on anyone they see as being up on themselves, having airs. Just the same, they admire you from afar, guaranteed."

He had touched a sensitive spot and made me recoil just a fraction. Is this what I had come to, needing the likes of this nobody to tell me that I was admired from afar. Yet I found myself taking comfort, poor comfort, but nonetheless comfort in his words. It was heartening, like a touch of weak sunshine on a bleak day. Privately I savoured those words and stored them away to help me cope with the days ahead, when I would have to face people whom I knew didn't have much time for me. I'd have to smile my well-mannered smile and then smile some more and absorb their overflowing grief and sympathy.

As all this went through my head, I sensed that Fred was watching me closely, like an animal assessing its prey, getting ready to pounce. Then he leaned into the table, closing the distance between us. I could see the earnestness in his eyes and smell the coffee on his breath.

"He was a real doctor," he said, "the people's doctor. Rich or poor, it made no difference. When someone needed him he was there. He couldn't pass a person on the street that was down and out without a kind word or a bit of help."

He squared his shoulders for a moment and pulled back. I thought he was about to end the conversation and leave. Instead he began tapping his fingers lightly on the tabletop. "I met him late one night on the stairs of a rooming house. Perfectly turned out as usual, his bag in hand." He shifted and turned away and with a backward wave of his hand appeared to dismiss the next thought. "You don't want to hear what was up there waiting for him." He shook his head confirming his decision. "I warned him but he went on up regardless. It was just his way, someone needed him." He raised his eyes. "I often wondered, Sylvia, if you knew about all he did."

"Did I know?" I took a deep breath, striving to retain my composure. "Tell me this. Have you ever stopped to consider whether Jack was paid for his services that night or, for that matter, the countless other nights when, as you say, 'someone needed him'? And who, may I ask, do you think was here when he arrived home smelling of 'what was up there'? Who do you think had to stretch the pittance he was paid, or, more often, not paid, for his services? There was no government health plan in those days, Fred. You appear to know all about his good deeds. Do you also know why he chose to place the needs of others ahead of those of his family?" I was ready to explode!

"He had a social conscience, Sylvia. In his book, access to medical help was a right not a privilege."

I managed to get control of myself but I can tell you, that night, I could have happily reached over and boxed Fred's ears for daring to presume that I did not know what was going on in my own house, for implying that my husband's family should not be his first priority. I had married a doctor with his eyes set on becoming a consultant but he changed his mind. I was never consulted. Did I know indeed! I reached for another cigarette.

My hand was trembling and I was furious to see that Fred had noticed. That I was even thinking about, never mind actually discussing such things with Fred, added a further spark to my anger. This little man who presumed to express his feelings to me, so openly, as if it was the most natural thing in the world, sat there quietly composed while I fumbled about, losing my temper and at a loss for words. The cheek of him to suggest that he knew more about my business than I did. Of course, rum had loosened his tongue but I knew no amount of alcohol would loosen my tongue and let me discuss my private life any further with this person. Still, I remember how it felt good at the time to feel anything at all, even anger.

Until that night, I don't think I had ever really understood the breadth and depth of Fred's connection to Jack. He knew Jack in ways that I never dreamed of. I can admit now that it made me jealous. I never understood what Jack saw in Fred. It had occurred to me that he was taking advantage of Jack's good nature; that he was a bit of a parasite. This is what was passing through my mind when Fred suddenly leaned in closer, removed his thick glasses and laid them on the table. As if seeing me for the first time, he scrutinized me carefully and then broached the subject of donating Jack's organs.

"Jack was very interested in the work being done in this area," he said. "He followed the progress being made in the medical magazines. It's what he'd want, Sylvia. That was his way; he gave what he had to those in need. There are so many in need. His organs are young and healthy and still working. From what you tell me, they are no good to him any-more."

The two whitish circles around his eyes glowed like pale moons. "Are you suggesting that I have Jack's body eviscerated like a dead chicken and the parts shipped in a cooler across the country to be planted inside any Tom, Dick or Harry who — "

"Yes I am." He sounded almost apologetic, yet forceful enough to demand my attention. "It may not be my place to say but I know it is what Jack would want. I am absolutely sure."

The audacity! But deep down, although I wouldn't dream of admit-ting it, I knew Fred was probably right.

Then he picked up his glasses, adjusted them on his nose, stood and retrieved his hat. "I apologize if I have offended you, Sylvia." He looked as he turned his hat slowly round and round on his fingers. "If you will excuse me now, I'll leave you in peace. Good night. Thank you for the coffee."

I watched, dumbfounded, as he went off down the stairs, not quite believing what had just transpired. *It is what he would want. I am absolutely sure.* How can he know better than me what Jack would want? How could he be so cocksure? It had not even crossed my mind, apart from when it was mentioned at the hospital. I heard the click-clack of claws coming slowly across the floor. They stopped a few feet away.

"I suppose you have an opinion too," I snapped. Max took a step closer and clawed the space between us with his outstretched paw. "No," I said, brushing him aside. "Go to bed."

I remember being overcome by panic, moments when I felt I was living outside of myself in some kind of insubstantial place. I had physically shrivelled into a tight ball that bounced sluggishly hither and thither, occasionally setting down in a spot I was sure was firm ground, only to find it was unstable. Then, I'd take off once more on a cloud of indecision, vacillating from one crazy space to another. I chain smoked and admonished myself for doing so and finally decided to drag myself upstairs to try to get some sleep.

I prayed that night, and I talked to Jack as if his head were there on the pillow beside me and I begged him to help me. While I waited for sleep to come, I watched the lonely clouds drift past in the night and I wondered if, once the beeping machine was silenced and the dancing line ceased to dance, would Jack's spirit drift by with the clouds as he left this world.

Once the idea of donating Jack's organs had been planted in my mind it simply would not go away. I had taken possession of the idea. Jack had mentioned this work in passing several times, but I had not discussed it with him as Fred obviously had. The pressure began to mount within me to make a decision. I sometimes experienced an odd feeling of real excitement and then all of a sudden this excitement would be swamped by feelings of guilt, even loathing. As all of this surged around inside of me I would try to rise above it, to find a solid place in my head where everything would be clear, where I could know for certain what I must do.

I was young then, young for my forty years, not used to making decisions — at least not important decisions. They had always been made for me but this time, the decision was mine and mine alone.

Out of all the pain and confusion that surrounded me during those few days, donating Jack's organs was the only thing that made any real sense. It lifted my spirits and allowed me to focus on something specific. When eventually I spoke with the people concerned, they were straightforward and kind, attentive to my concerns. There was an element of urgency in their approach but at no time was I pressured. Once I learned that Jack's body would be returned to me within twenty-four hours, outwardly intact but minus his donated organs, I felt a great sense of relief and a certainty that this was the right decision. I could dress him in his best suit of clothes with his hair combed neatly and a white handkerchief in his breast pocket and he would look much the same as he always did. I could have a proper wake and burial where I could take my place by his body, knowing that part of him still lived on in the real world.

Dealing with the James and Claire, telling them of my decision to shut down the machines that allowed their father to continue breathing and to donate his organs, was very difficult. I remember feeling painfully inadequate, totally at a loss to find the words I needed. I thought about how Jack would deal with the situation if things were reversed. I could see him, holding them, explaining every detail, answering all their questions, kissing away their tears, all the things I wanted to do but could not do so comfortably. So I ushered them into the car and drove to the hospital, anxious to get it over and done with as quickly as possible. Outside his room, I tried to herd them towards the inevitable. But Claire was resisting, surreptitiously edging closer to her brother, reaching for his hand.

"I can take care of this, Mother," he said.

"It's got to be done, James."

"We need private time with Dad, Mother."

"Yes, of course. Of course you do."

Why had this not occurred to me? I looked around looking for — I don't know what, and then remembered the special waiting room and went to find it.

It was empty. Shiny new red chairs lined the walls — a smell of new vinyl, everything back in order. A tall green artificial plant stood in the corner, a picture from some sunny place hung on the wall. Where was the young couple? Had everything changed for them too? Suddenly it came to me that I had not been back here to see Jack during the past two days, and that my children had not been to see their father.

There in that red vinyl room, I cried and cried uncontrollably. I was twelve years old again. I wanted to see Granny Bolfe one last time before they took her away forever but my father whispered in my ear — a hard cold whisper — "Control yourself, you silly girl. I don't want you in there making a fool of yourself."

And then I was running: down the stairs, through the hall, out into the cold, to the barn, running, running. I never saw Granny again.

Money — either too much or too little — was at the root of many of my problems. Things came and went because of money. Growing up in Ireland, want had no reality for me. It was something others dealt with, but not Sylvia Bolfe-Carter. I was blind to the needs of others. And so, my expectations of what to expect of life in this new world were distorted and unrealistic. I constantly looked for more because I believed that was my right, but what I got was never enough.

When I had arrived in this strange and desolate place — and it was just that — I was raw and inexperienced. I lived in a constant state of disbelief, never quite knowing who I was or what I should or should not be doing or saying. "When does spring come?" I'd ask. "Is it always like this, this constant, rain, drizzle and fog? Why does your mother cook the beef until it turns grey? Where are all the restaurants?" It was all a mystery to me.

I began to fight back trying desperately to understand, to find a place where I could feel comfortable and secure. I suppose I tried too hard or went about it the wrong way because it didn't work. I created enemies at every turn. I'm not even sure if I truly believe it all, but I do accept that I had a warped sense of what was rightfully my due. These days they call it entitlement and it's quite common, but back then it was not an option for me, not in Jack's social circle. His solution was to throw a few salty platitudes my way: "Leave your foolish pretentions at the door and get on with life," and "You suffer from delusions of grandeur." Easy for him to talk with his close circle of family, friends and a well-established lifestyle.

It was a closed circle and entry, if that was what one wanted, had to be earned. One had to learn the rules, and to me, those rules were not always acceptable. I just wanted to be me. Was that so much to ask, to hold on to my own identity? I thought not. I stubbornly remained an outsider.

So when want suddenly became my new reality, advice, salty or otherwise, was scarce. I had no place to go and no one to turn to.

When I found out that Jack's insurance coverage was totally inadequate for our needs, problems began to emerge at every turn. I was swamped with information: requests for signatures on bank accounts, deeds for the house, government forms to be filled in. I had no one to turn to for help. So, I ignored them — pretended that they did not exist. I refused to answer the door. I allowed the phone to ring endlessly. I had no wish to see or be seen by anyone. I just lived and relived that terrible day searching for anything, any small detail, that might clear the confusion and disbelief and bring me back to where I had been. I posed impossible questions and searched for answers that were not there. I tried to piece together fragments of information but always ended up more broken and exhausted than before.

I lost track of time and days. Fred came and went through the side door and the children were left to fend for themselves. James returned to school in Quebec; Claire began to spend all of her time at her friend's house and soon she was sleeping there. I just shut down completely.

One day I decided to go and find Claire after school.

"I think you should come back now," I said, standing on the pavement outside of her school.

"Why?"

"Because that is where you belong."

"Why?" she repeated.

"It is where you live."

"I don't want to live there anymore." She said this in such a matter of fact way that all I could do was stare as she hurried away to catch up with her friends.

She turned once and waved; a childish, guilty little wave, her fingers swishing back and forth as if wiping away my image. I watched helpless until she disappeared in the crowd and then I turned and headed back to the house.

Max met me at the door and for the first time since Jack died I paid attention to him. I stroked his smooth head and told him that Claire didn't want to be with us anymore. He didn't react so I let him be and went to get him some food and water. His bowls were already full. Fred, I realized, had taken over the job of caring for our dog.

The next day I went to Claire's friend's house to speak with her mother.

"She's had a terrible shock," she said, "losing her dad like that, so suddenly." The woman's tone suggested that I didn't understand.

I was ushered into the kitchen. Two loaves of newly baked bread on the kitchen counter sent out their particular message of contentment.

"Give her some time, Sylvia. She is such a sensitive girl. She seems to be happy here for now. Claire is very welcome to stay for a while."

I wanted to inform the woman, Elizabeth Foster, that I too had had a shock, that my house was empty, my husband dead, my children gone, that I needed my daughter with me. I wanted to pick up the damn bread and…

"You can have one, if you like," she said.

Suddenly, I was tired and cold and wanted to be out of there. I thanked her for her kindness to Claire and left with the warm bread wrapped in a brown paper bag and tucked under my arm.

"Don't you worry about Claire," she said, before closing the door behind me. "Just take care of yourself. I'll call you soon, Sylvia."

When I got home, Max came ambling across the kitchen floor looking forlorn and lost. I reached out to touch him, a sob rising in the back of my throat and when I felt the rough stroke of his tongue on my hand I dropped to my knees and cradled his head to my bruised self. From then on Max slept on the floor in my room. Through the empty nights I lay awake listening to the sound of his steady breathing and the occasional convulsive shudder as he chased rabbits in his dreams.

KATE EVANS

47

A day or two later, Elizabeth Foster phoned to invite me to supper with the family. I told her I was already invited out, which was untrue. I asked to speak with Claire but the girls weren't home. "They are working on a project at school," she said cheerily. "I'll ask her to call you when she gets home."

Claire never did call.

It was around that time that I began wandering during the day. I could not sit still so I walked up and down the web of streets and alleyways in the city: Job's Cove, Baird's Cove, Barter's Hill, Nunnery Row — one seemed to run into the next. I trudged along without direction or purpose, detouring into churches and other public places when I needed rest or shelter. Rain, wind and sun weighed on my shoulders and became a part of my grief. I was on the move but going nowhere, my eyes looking straight ahead in case anyone should attempt to stop me and make conversation. It was the only way I could keep the terror inside me at bay.

So many times I thought I saw Jack across the street or getting into a car but he'd disappear before I got there. Once I walked all the way to Mount Pearl, certain I had seen him ahead bobbing in and out of traffic. When I began to flag with exhaustion I looked around and didn't know where I was. Someone directed me back to St. John's. When people who looked vaguely familiar approached me, I looked in the opposite direction.

I began to go wherever my feet took me. I came on some of the old trails outside the city and followed the tracks across the cliffs. I had long conversations with myself, complaining about the weather, the harsh landscape, the cold, the wind, this damn unforgiving country. I had flights of fantasy that took me back to Ireland where, in my mind, it was always spring — the hedgerows dewy soft with snowdrops, the haze of bluebells through the woods. Those days, dreams of Kilgraney filled me with wistful longing and the life I once had.

The persistent screeching of gulls or a cutting blast of wind usually brought me back to reality and the "if only" stage quickly followed. If only I hadn't been so impulsive, if only we had stayed in Ireland, Jack and me, if only my parents had got to know Jack better, if only I had tried to coax my father around as James had suggested. If only Daddy had tried to understand. Then it was time to turn on Jack, to blame him for my predicament, to curse his impatience to return to Newfoundland, "God's country," he'd say as if talking about heaven on earth.

It never occurred to me to tell anyone where I was going or to think that what I was doing was dangerous until, one day, I was stopped along a trail by a rough-looking fellow who tried to make conversation with me. In an instant I assumed my haughty, belligerent persona. "Get out of my way," I said as I pushed past him with a purposeful stride, forcing him to step aside. I quickened my pace, determined to put distance between us, but his jeering reached me on the wind.

"Ha, ha, ye don't know me now ye whore, but last night…" The rest was lost on the wind.

Thankfully he didn't persist or follow me but it gave me a jolt. After that I decided to take Max with me on my rambles. It turned out to be a good decision. He was pleased, even excited, to come along and I believe his company kept me sane. He soon came to expect the daily event and was usually just ahead of me to the door, his tail thumping back and forth.

The gulls swooping in over the cliffs bothered him more than me, their screeching whipping him into frenzy, prompting me to call out praise and encouragement as he charged in all directions trying to catch them. Most of the time he walked by my side, every so often disappearing into the scrubby brush but never straying too far. I started to carry treats in one pocket and, later on, a snack for myself in another. Until then I had never thought of eating on my rambles unless I passed a gas station or a small shop where I might stop and purchase a chocolate bar. But I began to look forward to a break, to anticipate a bite to eat in the lea of a large boulder or behind a hillock with Max, warm and panting tucked in by my side.

"I'm frightened, Max," I whispered one day. "I am so frightened."

He poked his nose under my arm so that I was forced to cradle his head against my thigh. "The brown envelopes, Max, the bills," I said. "They have to be paid. I don't know what to do. Jack always paid the bills.

He always told me not to worry, that he would take care of everything. And he did, I suppose."

The smooth pulsating feel of the dog's belly beneath my hand made me feel there was something real and alive beside me, listening to my concerns. "What am I to do, Max? I cannot deal with it, yet I know that I must. Jack has deserted us, Max. Those brown envelopes make me angry." I had taken to opening the envelopes and scanning the contents. If I saw any sign of red ink or the word *Urgent* stamped on the sheet, I ripped it up immediately and threw it away. "Max, sometimes I feel unhinged, I can't help myself. We loved each other so much. We were lovers, always. Why did he do this to me?" I would look into Max's eyes, wondering if he could comprehend what I was saying. "I must do something, Max. We cannot keep walking forever and going nowhere."

I liked to think Max understood my rants. When he snuggled closer, pushing hard against the ground with his hind legs to maintain his position, I saw that as a sign to continue and then I'd carefully explain to him how the white envelopes are different, that they are cards and letters of sympathy. How every day, I'd look amongst them for an Irish postmark. How I wrote to my father about Jack's death three months ago and still hadn't heard back from him, not a word, not even a card.

How foolish it seems now but these conversations with Max helped me. I had no one to talk to and I was lonely. I knew that Mummy was gone. Not that she would have listened to my problems or have any advice to offer, but people do turn to mothers in times of need. Weeks after she died, I had a letter from a solicitor to say that I had inherited her jewelry. Did she think that was what I wanted from her? I have never claimed it. Why should I bother with her bits of glitter. They mean nothing to me. She never listened to my concerns, never took my part, never held me in her arms. She had no interest in horses, never attended a meet, not even the big important ones. I longed for her approval and praise. It was as if I didn't exist. Life is strange, all that effort, giving birth, raising a child, and then to lose interest just like that. I suppose that is how life goes ....To everything there is a season ... and I suppose my season has passed or will come or — whatever.

Eventually I realized there was neither space nor time for grief in my life. Things were out of hand. The house was filthy, my bed unmade, dog hair everywhere, Claire gone, information pouring in telling me what I should do, what I must do. I could no longer pander to my desire for isolation.

I mustered up the courage to phone James at school to explain that not only would his sister not be joining him at school in Quebec in September, but that he could no longer stay there beyond the end of term. He paused for a moment to absorb the news and then laughed lightly, saying, "Mother, just swallow your pride and phone your father. Turn on the tears and he'll cough up for his grandchildren."

I was shocked that he was so aware of my problems and that he had a solution already worked out. I had never mentioned this to him; he had never seen the bills on the kitchen table. But he knew. I was picturing him at the other end of the phone in a draughty school corridor, sensing the whiff of impatience and criticism in his attitude. This was certainly not what I had hoped for or expected.

"You don't understand," I said. "You know nothing about my family situation."

"There are ways and means, Mother. Trust me. We are his only grandchildren."

I was too ashamed to admit that only a few days ago I had cautiously entertained the idea of writing to my father again and asking for help. I wasn't penniless but I was fast approaching a crisis. But when I recalled my final conversation with my father and the sharp stab of his cruel dismissal, I was unable to put pen to paper. I thought of telling James this but could not bring myself to disclose this very personal information over the phone. James was always prepared to fight for what he wanted and I knew that simply accepting my decision just like that was not his way. I was also sure that he knew more than I did about my family. So I posed the next question carefully.

"You are right, James, your grandfather is a wealthy man or was at one time. Do you have news of him?"

James, to my utter astonishment said, "Yes," and went on to tell me in a very matter-of-fact voice that he was in touch with my brother. He had had a letter and had spoken with him on the phone in Oxford. It seems that at his school there was a young lad, a friend, from England. The boy's father was a professor at Oxford and was on sabbatical in Canada. He knew my brother. The news was that my clever brother was now a full professor and a leading authority on, "some poet or other." He had never married.

"So Mother, as I said, no other grandchildren."

I had an immediate image of a bookish middle-aged man, slightly pompous, espousing to a room full of students his theories on John Donne and then, goodness me, speaking with my son, James.

"Why didn't you tell me this? I had a right to know," I said.

"Because he particularly asked me not to."

"Why? I would like to hear from my brother."

"Then write to him. He is at Oxford University."

It took me quite a while to digest this information and I have to say I found it to be very disconcerting. I was pleased to hear the unexpected news of my brother, yet I felt a strange sense of disquietude. What if he phoned or wrote to me? It was over twenty years since I had seen him. We were young and inexperienced then and had little in common. To be middle aged and looking for family connections was daunting. What could I possibly have to say to him and how could I conceal or reveal my present situation? My pride dictated that this was not the time. I had to wait until things had settled down.

Needless to say, when I approached Claire to tell her the situation, I did so very gingerly. James's reaction had been a shock and there was no reason to believe that Claire's would be otherwise. True to form she just shrugged and said she didn't want to go to any snobby private school anyway and went about her business, doing well at school and seeing her friends.

At my insistence, she had come back to live with me. She had, while away, moved into adolescence with speed and determination. I noticed a change in her attitude, a new independence and a distinct move away from the status quo. There were occasional outbursts of anger, the usual kind of modern teenage behaviour; something I was not used to and declared to be unacceptable. She spoke to me in a disparaging way as if she was weary of my ineptitude and dithering. She began trading in her good clothes for rubbish in the second-hand shops and borrowing her friend's things even though they didn't really fit properly.

"Don't be silly, Mummy," she said when I commented on her dishevelled appearance. "It's my new poor-girl look. That's life now." She walked away, but flung another rather cutting comment my way as she left. "Have you looked at yourself recently?"

I hadn't.

Another month went by and I did nothing. Jack had been dead for over three months. I had regained some measure of control but continued to be extremely agitated and erratic in my behaviour. The breaking point came one night when I discovered that Claire was not in her room asleep as I had thought. A pair of scissors lay on the floor and tufts of mousey blond hair lay all over the floor. It was two o'clock in the morning and she was gone. I threw a coat on over my nightdress and went to look for her. I had no idea where to look, however, so I drove around the deserted streets aimlessly. I thought I saw her disappear up a laneway but by the time I had parked the car and run to the spot, she had disappeared. Later when I pulled into the driveway, the light was on in the kitchen. I burst through the door in a torrent of fury. Fred was standing in the kitchen like he owned the place.

"What do you want?"

"I thought you'd need a hot drink."

"Claire is missing."

"She's home now. She's upstairs asleep."

I saw a glass on the table, brown cloves floating in an inch of pale liquid, the honey jar sitting alongside, steam rising from the kettle on the stove. I imagined the hot liquid scalding my innards. I wanted it desperately — two, three, four of them — but what to do? So, I did what I usually did at times like that; I threw a few vicious words in Fred's direction, effectively blocking out any conversation. He paid no attention to me, just placed a long metal spoon in the glass, poured hot water from the kettle, added a teaspoon of honey and pushed the drink across the table. The smell of cloves reached me on the steam. I closed my eyes and inhaled.

"I suggest you have a hot bath," he said, as he turned to leave.

"Stay! Please stay." That was what I wanted to say, but I'm not sure if the words ever left my lips or if he just didn't hear me, or if he chose to ignore me. He kept on going, each step making an empty thud on the wooden stairs.

I reached for a chair and sat down. The house seemed strangely peaceful. Claire was safe and Fred had cared enough to wait up and be sure that I too was safe. I wondered if Claire had found whatever it was she'd gone out looking for.

And me, I was hurting in places unknown, places I could not name, places deep inside of me that seemed to call out. But just then I felt secure in my own house. Steam rose from the glass on the table and the cloves smelled of winter. I picked up the glass and headed for the stairs and a hot bath, spent.

I never questioned or examined what had all taken place that night but something had changed inside of me. I had quietly slipped into a new place.

I found out much later that Fred had taken it upon himself to phone James at school and suggest that he come home right away and help sort things out. James did, and with Fred's help some sense of order was restored to the household.

It was around this time that Claire had her first panic attack. I was sorting some bills with James in the kitchen when we heard a loud thump coming from upstairs. James was halfway up the stairs while I was still at the table wondering what the noise was. It was the urgency in his movement, as if he had somehow expected an emergency that made me move. Claire's bedroom door was open and James was kneeling on the floor beside her. She was red in the face and sweating, her hands trembling, holding her throat and gasping for breath. He had ripped open her shirt and was lifting her head and shoulders off the floor. Her chest and neck were bright red.

"Call an ambulance. Now!" It was an order.

I suppose I didn't move right away or quickly enough, because he screamed at me.

"9-1-1. Now! She's having a heart attack."

Of course it wasn't a heart attack — but it certainly gave us a turn. It was James who gathered all the details of what to do should the same thing happen again. I was profoundly shaken by the incident and it brought back terrible memories of the day Jack died. Claire, however, seemed to take on a new kind of calm.

"You are my saviour, James," I heard her say to him after that incident.

Under James's guidance and care, her attacks on me became less virulent although she did continue to have panic attacks from time to time, but rarely as severe as the first time.

James seemed to have matured beyond his years; he taught me how to cope with Claire and her attacks. He seemed to instinctively understand Clair's needs and saw clearly what had to be done. He made things work. I suppose that is why I always trusted him so absolutely, even when I shouldn't have.

James returned to school and Fred stepped decisively out of the shadows and became a real presence in our lives. He showed up unexpectedly at crucial moments to identify and defuse tricky situations or to lend a helping hand. His influence was felt in several areas and Claire frequently commented, "Fred likes it," or "Fred thinks," or "ask Fred..." He took on the task of clearing the car of snow and ice, took out garbage without being asked. One day as winter approached, he suggested I have my car winterized and offered to see to it.

"What do you mean *winterized*?"

"Remove the tires, add antifreeze —"

"No need to do that. Jack had the car serviced in spring."

"Sylvia, if you don't winterize, with the first fall of snow you'll be lucky to get out of the driveway and if you do, you'll take off down Prescott Street like a kid on a sled and if you survive that jaunt, you'll have to push her back up. Now, I can do that for you."

"Did Jack do that, that winter thing?"

"Yes."

I was glad then to accept his offer. As time passed I felt a need to place Fred more accurately in the framework of our household and basically evaluate his position, if that was possible. I thought about this and decided that I needed to see where Fred lived. I convinced myself that it would help me get to know the man a little better. I realize now that I should have simply knocked on his door and found a respectful way to be invited in, but instead, one day I watched for his regular departure around noon. It was his custom to go to McMurdo's lunch counter every day for soup and a sandwich. This was *the* spot in the city for a cheap lunch and an update on the latest news and gossip. I crept down the stairs to the basement like an intruder to have a quick peek. That was my intention — to have a quick peek. But I got carried away.

The door to his room was closed. Either out of politeness, or in case by some quirk of fate he happened to be still inside, I knocked and waited before turning the handle. Once inside I was on high alert looking for I don't know what: clues, tell-tale signs, anything that might give me an insight into the man who lived in the basement.

My first impressions were of a drab, grey room that begged for a breath of fresh air. There was the faint smell of a cat in the room but there was no cat or litter box to be seen, but I recalled seeing a scrawny, beige cat lurking around the basement door from time to time as if expecting to be admitted. The next thing I noticed was that every square inch of wall was covered with drawings — pencil, charcoal, black ink, and no colour in any of it.

Directly opposite the door was a single, iron-framed bed placed lengthwise along the wall. The bed was unmade and the presence of some hair on the cover suggested that the cat was a nighttime guest. The slight depression on the pillow marked where his head had been. The thin quilt was thrown back at one corner. A small worn mat lay on the bare floor. High on the wall there was a small, rectangular window and underneath a makeshift table made of cement block and plywood. An assortment of pencils and pens of various sizes and shapes, some neatly sharpened others worn down to a stump, lay on the table, others were stacked points up in a *Campbell's Beef Stew* can. There was paper, scraps and sheets, a soft, white rectangular eraser, badly smudged, a bottle of black ink, stain marks on the plywood tabletop, half-finished drawings set aside, coloured pencils. Books and magazines lying all over the floor.

I moved very cautiously, afraid to make a sound, and went to examine the sketches on the wall behind me. The light was so poor I had trouble seeing but I didn't dare turn on the light.

I was face to face with two large drawings, both of women: one from behind, the curve of her shoulder and upper arm, the face in half profile; the other, a frontal view of a heavy-set torso, large breasts, an ample role of belly fat; the nipples pale and firm like ripening raspberries. I leaned in to take a closer look and noticed that one aureole was worked in a network of spidery pencil lines and the other in light shading. There was another face — this one stared back at me with hard defiant eyes. I shifted position. There were numerous detailed drawings of hands and feet. Hands clenched, extended, holding objects, old and sinewy long hard nails, claw-like, working hands, beautiful hands. The feet were mostly bony and hard; veins and tendons bulging as if bearing a lot of weight. They all looked like the same foot, just different aspects. All of these were carefully worked in pencil, charcoal or ink. Had Fred walked into the room at that moment, I might have said over my shoulder, "These are remarkably detailed."

Then something surprising caught my eye; a rather beautiful, wedge-shaped, cheese dish sitting on a low wooden stool in a corner. It was startling in so far as it looked completely out of place in the shabby room. It was ceramic, pale yellow in colour and textured throughout. The handle on the cover and along the edge of the plate was lavishly decorated with small orange poppies, red and blue fruits with touches of green foliage. In the center of the cover was a sheaf of golden wheat. I immediately recognized it as a Clarice Cliff, a highly skilled potter from the early 1900s. My mother had been a collector. This particular piece was from the Wheat Sheaf series. I lifted the lid. The smell was overpowering. The remains of a large wedge of cheese, bearded and discoloured, looked back at me. I dropped the lid with a loud clunk. I should have left then, but curiosity got the better of me.

A pile of papers and sketch pads in a corner caught my eye. I promised myself I would just glance at them, no more. Then I saw my name written neatly in black ink on the blue cover of a folder. I had to take a closer look.

There were numerous pencil drawings, some just quick sketches, but others were complete portraits in fine and significant detail, mostly in charcoal or pencil with touches of colour, all quite different but clearly, I was the subject. What I saw at a glance that day, as I turned the pages, was that the drawings appeared to catalogue certain times in my life; times and occasions that I could, in some instances, identify. There I was, sequestered between sheets of tissue, disdainful, happy, uncertain, afraid, angry, unsure, wonderfully elegant, heavy with sorrow, skeptical — a myriad of emotions and experiences etched on thick white paper.

One in particular is imprinted in my memory. I saw little of the detail at first. I remember a bleak landscape; a skim of frost covered everything. There was a thin strip of endless road. But when I looked carefully I saw how the surface of the road was rough and muscled, the edges cracked and hard. The bare, black trees were rooted to the horizon and the match stick house in the distance was totally devoid of features. It was barren and empty. Although I can no longer see this detail, I remember it clearly and it still sends a shiver through me. The woman who was standing on the road, at the forefront of the picture was me. I know it was me. The full face was not shown but a frightened eye looked backwards, burning like a hot tar bubble. Fred chose to dress me in a long, black overcoat and my head was covered in a close fitting black peaked cap. My feet were large and bare and web-like and my arms hung from my shoulders close to my sides and ended in narrow, pointed, feathery tips. He had depicted me as a birdlike creature, a crow or a raven. He called the picture *Nether World*. It is a disturbing and surreal piece — one that I wanted to forget but never could.

I dropped the folder. I may have cried out as I ran from the room. But I recall startling the dog as I flew through the kitchen, taking the stairs two at a time. Max sprang into action, overtaking me on the stairs and getting to the bedroom ahead of me before I closed the door. I curled into a knot on the bed and tried to shut out the world. He waited and eventually drew closer, slowly placing one paw on the edge of the bed. I knew he was there, knew what he was suggesting and when I eventually opened an eye to acknowledge his presence, he carefully placed the other paw beside the first one. He waited and watched and when I patted the covers he jumped onto the bed, expertly circling his body into the hollow curve of my back.

"I have become a dark creature," I told him.

Perhaps it was shock at what I had seen or shame because what I had done was unforgivable, but after that, I thought Fred looked at me in a different way, a knowing way that made me uncomfortable. By snooping, I had been forced to face an uncomfortable reality.

Shortly thereafter, I picked up the phone and made an appointment to see the bank manager. When I went about organizing myself for the ordeal, I realized how much weight I had lost. My best suit, a fine black wool, no longer fit me. I pinched in the waist of the skirt and secured it with a safety pin. The jacket, I hoped, would hide the tuck; with the help of a pretty blouse it would look fine. The jacket covered the tuck but it hung on my skinny shoulders as if on a wire coat hanger. The image was not encouraging. Head up, shoulders back... Granny's solution. I allowed myself a moment of reflection but at the first hint of self-pity and more tears, I went into a frenzy of activity, scurrying to and fro, searching the closet, pulling out every stitch of clothing that presented any possibility. I settled on a deep aqua sweater, a little too heavy for under the suit but the colour was better and it bulked me up. By then I was running late so I plonked myself in front of the mirror and leaned in to take a closer look at my face. I had acquired a ruddy, weathered hue. A cluster of freckles, like dust motes, spread across the bridge of my nose and across the top of my cheeks. Anger sat tightly around my mouth and when I added a bright slash of lipstick, tiny lines appeared that had not been there before. My hair was long and straggly so I coaxed it into a tight chignon and pulled out a few wispy strands to soften the look. A pair of black Italian-leather shoes that I had bought the previous year at Parker and Monroe, and I was ready.

Mr. William Holmes, the Royal Bank Manager, addressed me as Mrs. Drodge. I had never met the man before, so I appreciated his businesslike manner. He had a huge dome-like head with scant hair combed flat to his skull. His pale face had a purplish tinge around the cheeks and nose which put me in mind of a waxed turnip. He came from behind his desk to greet me and offered his condolences in a brief but appropriate manner, his quiet tone suggesting genuine sincerity and then, thankfully, it was straight to business.

"How may I help you?" He placed his forearms on his desk locking his fingers together and focused his full attention on me.

I felt utterly vacant inside, my plan gone. I remember being fixated on the white starched cuffs of his shirt that appeared just below his jacket sleeve and they reminded me of Jack. I forced myself not to become emotional. I assumed what I hoped was a confident pose and waited, feeding on the air of professionalism in the room.

"How may I be of assistance, Mrs. Drodge?"

I breathed deeply but quietly and began. "Since my husband died, our affairs have been terribly neglected." My voice sounded strange to my ear somehow, more like Granny. "Jack always looked after all our financial affairs. I hardly know how to write a cheque. You see, I never had to. I grew up…" This was not part of the plan. The words were becoming jumbled, getting lost. I took a deep breath.

"I'm very much out of touch with these matters and would be glad of your advice."

"I understand, Mrs. Drodge. This often happens when one loses a spouse so suddenly. There is no time for planning."

He looked right at me then, a quiet introspective look, but I knew in that moment he was well aware of my situation. He knew all about me, my family, my financial problems, my wanderings, my reduced circumstances. I reached furtively for the safety pin that held my skirt in place just in case it was showing and in that same instant I realized half of the town also knew what he knew.

He then began to list my assets: a small insurance policy, a mortgage-free house and a plumbing business that Jack had inherited from his father's estate.

"The business provides a small income, which is deposited directly into the bank. The financial side is handled by a Mr. Penny, an accountant and a family friend, I believe." He wrote the name and phone number on a sheet of paper and passed it across the table. He allowed me a moment to digest this information and then continued. "You are aware, I expect, that a Mr. McCarthy has been running the business since Mr. Drodge Senior died. He has been there for many years and was old Mr. Drodge's trusted employee. He is a good man, but I understand the business has been going downhill in the last few years. It is not an ideal situation." He spoke quietly.

"My husband had no interest in the business," I said, "and I never paid any attention to what went on there. His intention was to sell it. I don't even know where the business is located and I have no interest in getting involved."

"May I inquire as to your background, Mrs. Drodge? Your working background, that is."

I thought about this for a moment. "I could take a horse to a top-notch show — and inspire my teammates, too, when necessary. We would prance and dance our way with style and precision to the top of the ratings and I would bring home the hardware."

He raised his eyebrows and thrust his lower lip forward into a thoughtful pout. "Team work," he said, pulling at his lower lip, "skill, discipline, determination, hard work, Mrs. Drodge, all very important qualities."

His words stirred within me a well of confidence that made me blush with pride. "I was good with horses, Mr. Holmes, very good," I said, pleased that he had not dismissed my skills as trivial. "My father had planned for me to take over the family stud farm in Ireland. As a means to that end he sent me to university to study commerce but I only completed two years. That was a long time ago, before I met Jack."

There was a moment of silent introspection as he tapped lightly with the point of his pencil on his desk. A shinny, pinkish spot showed on top of his head where his hair was thinning. "Mrs. Drodge, you now own a business," he said, meeting my eye. "I think you should consider getting involved in developing that business." He leaned back in his chair and regarded me with a steady gaze. I remember thinking, *the man is serious!*

"I intend to sell the business," I said with a note of finality.

"You might consider chatting with your accountant before making such a decision. It was once a thriving operation. Maybe you can tidy things up there before you decide to sell. At least get it in better shape before putting it on the market. If that is what you wish, of course."

"Me?"

"You are obviously a very able woman, Mrs. Drodge. The question is, do you want to?"

Following the meeting with Mr. Holmes I felt totally upended. I had not considered for one moment that it was my job to fix my problem. I foolishly thought that someone, like the bank manager, could come up with a plan, implement it and so set me on a course to security and prosperity. That was how I thought things should work. Suggesting I become involved in any way with selling plumbing supplies was not my intention. It was out of the question.

Outside, I got in the car and drove with no destination in mind. I wanted to put as much distance between me and the bank as possible. I ended up that day at Cape Spear about ten miles outside of St. John's.

When I look back now, I wonder what drove me to that place on that day. On the map it's the closest point to Ireland in the whole of North America, but that was not the reason. I was looking for Jack. I needed him near me. This was the place where we went to be alone. In the early years of our marriage, it was a regular haunt. Sometimes it was the stillness of a beautiful summer night when the foxes ran freely along the grassy ledges, but more often than not it was the unbridled fury of the surf that coaxed us to drive the winding road on a wild, stormy night. We'd sit shivering on a high rocky promontory to watch and wait for our wave, the seventh one, the big one. We were like a couple of kids, tucked in together, cheering wildly, relishing the danger, on the ready, as the wall of shiny blackness gathered speed and headed directly for us. Momentary panic and then the wall collapsed and came crashing down in a great arc of freezing white spray on the jagged rocks. When the damp and cold settled into the very marrow of our bones, only then did we struggle to our feet and stumble to the car where we fed on salty kisses before heading back home to do battle with the storm within us.

Here I go, off on a flight of fantasy again but on that day there was a storm howling in my head and all I wanted was shelter from the terror within me. I wanted to wipe out the present, and be in the past. I must have succeeded because I remember nothing about that particular trip to Cape Spear, not the weather, the conditions, what I did there, how long I stayed. I just know I went there.

After that I purposefully went about shutting out the present, letting the past take over. It foraged around inside my head like a hungry grub looking for a juicy scrap to feed on. It wove a sticky web of malevolence and helplessness that frequently made Jack the target of my anger.

At night I lay awake, recalling over and over again things I no longer wanted to remember. It was mainly silly things that over the years had upset me. I dredged up incidents that had occurred and things about Jack that at one time had annoyed me. His obsession with "the guys," as he called them, was a big one: the hunting and fishing expeditions, his refusal to limit his time in their company or to modify his behaviour while with them had always been a source of aggravation. As I began to brood and seek ways to lay blame for my misfortune and shift responsibility, these memories burned inside of me with a vengeance. I couldn't stop myself. I conjured up vivid images of a bunch of grown men, cleaving to each other like overgrown school boys, exchanging well-worn stories and guzzling beer from bottles, something I had never seen him do when I first met him. Then he used a glass but now was teased by his friends when he did so.

The fishing trips that were so much a part of my romantic image of Newfoundland were not what I expected though we did enjoy a rather nice chalet on the Exploits River, owned by a friend of the family. It was comfortable, even luxurious, and quite to my taste. On one of these few visits we went with a group of six in the spring, three of Jack's friends and their wives. I enjoyed the fishing and proved quite adept with the rod, landing two very presentable salmon our first day out, one of which we had for dinner that evening, but I never could get used to dealing with the mosquitoes and at that time of year they were as big and plentiful as carpenter ants. No matter what I did they seemed to take great delight in tormenting me in particular. Jack had brought a kind of jacket made of net that covered my head and upper body somewhat, but the main damage was done at night when I lay unprotected in bed. In the morning I awoke with my right eye puffed and swollen and almost closed, my legs and arms bitten and bleeding where I had scratched.

Jack had always been so caring and attentive. In fact it was one of the things that endeared him to me when we first met but, over here, I had the impression that it wasn't the done thing. One had to be tough. Newfoundlanders were born and bred to be hardy and resilient, especially in the great outdoors. One had to cope with the forces of nature or whatever life dealt — to not just cope but laugh. It was a matter of back-slapping pride. Jack slipped easily into this mode when in the company of his male friends. Seeing my badly bitten puffy face, he casually produced from a cupboard an ancient bottle of calamine lotion, the cap chipped and rusted, the pink liquid caked around the top and to the sides.

"Come, my beauty," he joked, "let me soothe your tender flesh." He made a show of smacking his lips in anticipation, much to the amusement of the others, and began to shake the bottle.

"It's not funny, Jack. I need help, not hilarity." I felt so humiliated in front of his friends with my swollen eye and blotchy face. The day before, unlike the rest of the party, I arrived looking very country and chic. Now I stood there in the wretched kitchen bedraggled and unwashed trying desperately not to scratch and tear at my arms and legs and face and make it all worse. I wanted to run, get away, far away from the misery and humiliation. But I gritted my teeth, urging myself to be tough, to be strong and resilient and show them I was not a whining ninny. I so wanted Jack to be proud of me.

But the charade continued. Jack had begun to unscrew the cap slowly, walking towards me, making small coaxing noises as if I was a pet poodle. "Let's see what delicious spots have been invaded by those little devils."

It was then I reached out and with one swipe sent the bottle and contents flying across the floor. He looked angry before he laughed.

Somebody said "Ho, ho," as if anticipating a showdown — and there may have been a show if one of the women, Carol, hadn't come to my rescue.

"Come with me, Sylvia," she said gently. "I have some antihistamines in my bedroom."

I left in tears. Carol made a cold pack for my eye and suggested I rest and drink some fluids with the antihistamines. "This is a man's game," she confided, putting on her jacket. "Truth is, we're not really wanted on these trips. I don't know why I bother." She left quietly.

When I came back into the living room later on, the crowd, including Jack, was still on the river. I ignored the bottle and pink liquid spattered all over the floor and resolved that never again would I subject myself to such torture.

That incident at the chalet alienated me still further. I no longer went on those trips, so I began to spend many weekends at home, on my own, while Jack went with his friends. At nighttime, I dreamed Kilgraney back into my life. I fed on memories of cozy evenings surrounded by wealth and comfort: the hunt balls and parties, the life of fun and privilege in riding circles, when the biggest decision to be made was what to wear to the next event. The music, the dancing, the laughter filled my ears until reality set in and I could bring myself to be honest and recall how tired and bored I was with the whole scene until I met Jack Drodge.

His parents were another source of irritation. It irked me that he regularly deferred to them about things that were our affair. In my mind I rehashed incidents and fiery exchanges that at the time were distressing and hurtful, like the time he brought home a magnificent salmon from a fishing trip. I wanted to poach it in a court bouillon but he told me to call his mother and she would tell me what to do. Aware that once again I was being undermined, I lashed back, "Your mother wouldn't know a court bouillon from a bottle of Javex." In my fractured state of mind these memories served to whip me into a fury again and again.

It may seem trivial but I have to explain that the fact we were beholden to Jack's parents was a major problem for me — well, actually for us both. Jack's parents were older and this coupled with the fact that he was an only child and was born to them late in life made them very possessive. The pattern was that whatever Jack wanted Jack got. He didn't have to sweet-talk or very often even ask. Their generosity did not transfer to me. At Christmas time I was given things for the house: a toaster, towels, an ugly white tablecloth embroidered with yellow and purple pansies and trimmed with a yellow and purple crochet border. It was hideous.

"She is trying to please," Jack insisted. "She spent hours making it for you. Embroidery is her forte. Everyone knows that."

But I knew better. "It's was a slight," I said, "pure and simple."

"Or an imagined slight," he persisted.

Once for my birthday I got a big box all done up with bows and pretty flowered paper and, inside, a set of stainless mixing bowls. I was so annoyed that there and then, in her presence, I gave them to the children to play with.

The war of the gifts continued as long as she lived. We exchanged veiled insults and I delivered a few choice ones. Like the Victorian chamber pot I spotted in an antique shop. It had a lid and inside emblazoned on the bottom was a verse. *Use me well and keep me clean and I'll tell naught of what I have seen.* That took the smile off her face. James, to defuse the situation, suggested there might be a false bottom to the pot and a fortune from Victorian times concealed within. She promptly dropped it on the floor and the pot lay in smithereens. I was pleased but at the same time wondered what might have ensued if the trusty maker of the pot had in fact concealed a little surprise in a secret chamber! All might have been lost or much gained.

As the war between us continued I tried to rationalize this behaviour. I used to wonder if it was something I had said or done that had so alienated Jack's mother until one day, at a social gathering at their home, I overheard his mother say to a neighbour, "If only Jack had married a nice Newfoundland girl." From then on I had at least an idea as to why I was so pointedly ignored and made to feel like an outsider. Jack never did take my side, at least not to my knowledge, and if he did it never made any difference. I had stolen him. And she wanted him back.

Oh my! How I ranted in those days. I probably made his life a misery. When I talked to him about our feud, he said things like, "You must understand that I love you but I also love my parents."

A new wave of tenderness usually followed these arguments that lasted just about as long as the flowers that invariably made an appearance thereafter.

Although I was unhappy and often felt very isolated, I never stopped loving Jack. I sometimes looked inward to try and find a way to make things right. I told myself I was a snob, cold hearted and arrogant, but I couldn't bring myself to believe any of it was my fault. So with a nudge from Granny Bolfe, I usually shrugged off these notions and determined I had to be myself — and that I didn't have to change in order to please everyone. The truth was: I was jealous of their relationship, their love for each other, and their love of life.

So his mother and I continued to needle each other, a jab here and a jab there — a little like biting into a lemon and relishing the smarting taste. When Mrs. Drodge died twelve years into our marriage, I felt only relief.

At one time I decided what I was missing in my life was a horse. If Jack could go hunting and fishing, I could go riding. My horse had been an integral part of my life. Jack had settled in comfortably to what he had left behind, so why not provide accommodation for me. Excited by my idea, I broached the subject one night in bed. We had just made love and in the cozy warmth of his arms I thought this to be a good time.

He thought about it for a moment. "In a year or two, we'll look around for a good mount for you. In the meantime," he quipped, pulling me astride the broad plain of his body, "you'll have to settle for me."

I began to realize I was constantly in waiting mode: waiting for Jack to come home, waiting for Jack to make a decision, waiting for Jack to bring back the car, waiting for my horse. When he was offered a fellowship in Halifax to study Internal Medicine I was ecstatic until Jack turned it down. "I'm not ready just yet to start studying again. Besides I am enjoying family practice and glad to be home for now. Maybe in a year or two." Planning for the future was not on his agenda.

Looking back, it would have been an ideal time for Jack to finish his studies, the carefree student life away from everyone suited us both and I had it in my mind that I might finish my degree. We had no children and his father was more than willing to support us if Jack wanted to return to college. But the truth was, Jack had no interest in becoming a specialist of any kind.

With that clearly no longer on the agenda, I became pregnant with James and I realized the pattern of our lives had been set.

James was a fine baby, strong, healthy and even tempered. If only he hadn't required feeding and changing, things would have been fine. At Kilgraney, Nanny took care of the children. Nanny changed the nappies, did the cooing, the feeding, the bathing. I could not even imagine my mother holding a bottle to a baby, never mind exposing her breast and putting her nipple in its mouth. I had never seen my mother deal with mess of any kind. I soon realized this was what was expected of me. The whole business was, quite simply, beyond my experience. I couldn't even hold on to the little squirmer. When at all possible, I waited until Jack came home so he could change James and deal with the pile of dirty nappies in the bucket, waiting to be sluiced off. So every evening Jack was greeted at the door by James, screaming in protest, his face crimson with exertion. Jack could calm him in an instant, gently cleaning and powdering his red, raw bottom and saying, as he went about the job, "Mother can teach you. It's easy when you know how." But I wanted nothing to do with the whole business.

She came to the house shortly thereafter on Jack's instruction. One look at James's bottom and she turned on me. "He's your baby. Don't you care? He cannot help himself."

I asked her to leave but before she did she looked right at me and said to my face what I already knew.

"Jack should have married a girl from here who knows how to look after her family."

I remember my retort. "Just like you, I suppose." It made her eyes fill up and that pleased me.

However she did find us a nice Newfoundland girl. Rosie Barron had grown up in a large family and knew how to cope. At seventeen she knew all about the whole business of rearing and caring. When she left at five o'clock, I counted the minutes until Jack arrived home and took over. In spite of my best efforts, two years later, I became pregnant again and to my great relief, Rosie Barron coped as well with two children as with one. That was the trouble with all these people — they just seemed to cope with everything, could do everything: bake bread, pluck partridge, unblock sinks, 'put an arse in a cat', I heard someone once say. Often in such circumstances I stood by like a limp doll as Rosie Barron ran the household. She was unabashedly in her element. She could do it all and at the end of the day still smile. She did make one mistake, she managed to get herself pregnant before the year was out.

"She's not even a Catholic!" Was Jack's mother's comment on hearing of this state of affairs. But there she was, a good Protestant ballooning by the day.

I thought this turn of events would put a halt to Rosie Barron's gallop, but no, she was into the hospital, had her baby and back to work within a week, baby and all. Jack had what he always wanted: a house full of children and constant activity. He was in his element.

I had to get out and away from the noise and upheaval. I had played tennis from an early age and had been quite good on the court, so I joined the tennis club. I was an able contestant and in demand as both a singles and a doubles partner. Soon I was playing in tournaments and enjoying the competition. As winter approached I was invited to play bridge with some of the ladies, but I was not so comfortable with that situation. The rules I had learned were different, but I managed to play along and adapt. My life had settled into a kind of pattern that I found to be pleasing, although still not what I had envisaged.

As I became more involved in the social life of the city, I found the class system was more relaxed than when I had first arrived. Back then amongst the Protestant population there was a certain feeling of mistrust, even a cautious fear of the Catholic population, which was mostly of Irish extraction. I was Irish but an upper-class Protestant and that made me a bit of an enigma. Having married into a business that could be classified as trade, I was further misplaced, but now with Jack choosing to be the poor man's physician I was even more of a misfit. It took me a while to figure this out. In his case, using his medical skills to be of service to the poor didn't appear to warrant the right kind of recognition.

I have to admit this troubled me more than it would have most people. I craved recognition, longed to be invited to the right homes. Government House should have been within reach but even when the Catholic Lieutenant Governor's term was up and he was replaced by a Protestant, as was the custom at the time, there still was no invitation forthcoming. I just didn't fit the roster.

Yet when I finally found my way onto the tennis court, the various groups appeared to mix easily. There, I found, as in many other areas, it was skill and not social position that mattered. Power and money had shifted. Things had changed. Newfoundland was no longer an isolated colony. It was part of Canada and old norms had broken down. It was no longer so much about money and position but talent, ability and education.

You may be thinking now, how could this woman be so unaware, how could she live in a place and not see what was taking place all around her? The simple answer is that I did not want to see. I wanted life to be as I had imagined it. I wanted Jack to be a successful and brilliant consultant married to me, a woman of breeding. I wanted social standing in this place. Jack had no interest in such things. He cared nothing for position or standing and scoffed at the very idea. "Broaden your horizons, Sylvia," he suggested. "Find more worthwhile pursuits. The best apple is not always at the top of the tree."

To him it was all a load of nonsense. But I continued to look for what I thought to be my rightful place. The more I tried, the more I seemed to isolate myself. I became known as a social climber, which served to isolate me still more. Time passed me by. I could blame my upbringing, my youth, my inexperience but I can never excuse the fact that I had willfully cut myself off from the place where I had freely chosen to live because it hadn't lived up to my expectations.

I am admitting this now, but tomorrow I may not be so forthcoming and contrite.

Here I am still stuck in the same spot. Lynn Rose, the physiotherapist, has been and set up a therapy program for me. I cannot leave here until I can perform certain functions on my own. That means I have to get up and walk on my own from to A to B and use the stairs. I am more inclined to cooperate now but it is a tiresome carry-on and the woman is so impatient with me. You see, I don't like to be seen outside of my room shuffling along the corridors supported by this ridiculous looking walking cage with two wheels on the front legs, two flat tennis balls on the back legs so that I can push it along the floor as I go. What is the point when I can barely see where I'm going?

"Don't worry about that just now," she says. "I'll guide you."

Yes, but what then? Before she leaves I'm returned to my parking spot and off she goes.

How I ever managed to establish myself in the plumbing business is still a mystery to me. Radical change had been thrust upon me and I had to find a way to deal with it. I was tired of the empty life I had created for myself, tired of the whole business of being a Bolfe. Nobody here gave a damn about my lineage. In this place it had been a hindrance rather than a help. So perhaps this was a way to hoist myself out of the rut I had created. Had I inherited a different kind of business, something more to my liking, the solution would have been easier. James was right. Had I kept my head and been more circumspect in dealing with my father, I would be in line now for a sizable inheritance. I had been foolish and impulsive. So in this state of flux, my thoughts tumbled along in a torrent of change, my children frequently getting dragged along in the undertow. There were no real solutions, no answers, so I continued to struggle through those lonely, trying days, wondering always what to do and who to turn to.

I tried to keep the bank manager's advice to the forefront of my mind and see myself as an able woman. I coaxed myself with the notion of assuming a new look, of buying a professional wardrobe, taking on the role of business woman, but the thought of shopping at the dowdy stores on Water Street that peddled a family name, as if that alone guaranteed style and good taste, depressed me. The fact was, I had no idea how to prepare or what to expect from this new job I was supposed to take on.

One day I reached for the telephone book and looked up the address of James Drodge & Company Plumbing Supplies. I remember writing down the name and address, carefully forming every letter and number on a note pad as if writing an invitation to an event of some kind. I posted the handwritten note on the fridge in the kitchen in the hope that, over time, I might find inspiration or at least grow accustomed to the idea.

"What's that?" Claire asked.

"It's the location of the family business."

"And…?"

"I may have to get involved, to keep an eye on things," I said.

She had her back to me, her head in the refrigerator. She looked over her shoulder and held the door open with one hand.

"Becoming a Women's Libber, Mummy? I don't believe it. Did you see the Ogle March?"

Talk of the Ogle March was everywhere. I heard one woman in the supermarket refer to the participants as "castrating bitches." To my horror, women were burning bras, dumping girdles and high-heeled shoes and hair curlers and all manner of feminine accouterments into garbage bins and setting them alight. They even resorted to fondling and pinching men's bottoms. I thought it all to be utterly disgraceful. In fact, I felt quite indignant that they should presume to disrespect our gender in the name of all women. I wanted no part of it.

"Certainly not, Claire," I said. "I want to keep an eye on what is going on over there."

No longer interested in the contents, she closed the fridge and gave me her full attention.

"Jane's mother is going back to work. Mrs. Foster says that it's time for women to look beyond the dishes and laundry and get out into the real world. Even Mr. Crosbie agrees. He's advocating wage parity for women so she's jumping on the bandwagon."

"You mean, Mr. Crosbie, the minister of finance?" I said.

"Yes, Mummy."

"He is not the premier."

"No, but these days he is the one in government making the decisions."

"How do you know?" I wasn't used to having this kind of discussion with Claire.

"We were talking about it at school. These are interesting times for women. We don't want to be like our mothers."

I remember thinking: Claire has grown up, she's speaking to me like an adult. Days later, more cognizant of this fact, I discovered she had begun to menstruate. I had been unaware of this milestone. She had never mentioned it. She had also applied for a part-time job at Woolworths on Water Street, which was denied her because, at age fourteen, she was too young. But on her own initiative, she was making her own money tutoring some students in her class in math and science.

Three weeks passed before I found the courage to drive past the entrance to James Drodge & Company Plumbing Supplies.

A wide, leafy laneway off the main road led to what appeared to be a large clearing. As I edged past the entrance, I could see the side of a big grey building. Just then a truck came around the corner of the laneway and I sped away in case I was recognized or that I might, in a weak moment, pluck up the courage to drive up to the door to take a closer look at the property. I continued on down the street, my heart thumping, not sure if it was fear or excitement.

A few days later I drove across town again to the property. It was late evening. I hoped the business would be closed and I would be able to take stock of the place without being seen. However I found my access was barred by a metal barrier across the opening. I was annoyed. I was the owner. I should have a key. Next time I showed up, I resolved that I would have a key. It was a full week before I picked up the courage to return, this time in broad daylight. I parked in a secluded corner of the clearing, slid down in the seat like a skulking criminal and pulled my hat well down over my eyes and hair. I'm not sure why I felt so insecure and secretive — like a wilting plant gasping for food and water. I sat there for over an hour watching the comings and goings. There were three buildings surrounded by big mature trees: the main building was a large rectangular affair with grey wooden clapboard and a few stray windows set haphazardly in different areas. Three rickety concrete steps led to faded, double doors. A sign overhead said CUSTOMER ENTRANCE. To the back and side I could see two fair-sized sheds. There was activity in and around the nearest shed, men busy unloading copper piping from a large delivery van. I could hear the loud clanging of metal even at a distance with the car windows closed. A woman appeared at the double doors, called out something to the men and disappeared inside. One man left the group, walked towards the building and went inside. I wanted to get out of the car, walk purposefully to the concrete steps, follow him through the double doors and introduce myself but I couldn't bring myself to move. I tried to picture what was behind those doors, what to say if I was mistaken for a customer. I should have phoned first and spoken to Mr. McCarthy and set up a meeting. I took a deep breath, turned the key in the ignition and drove away, determined to approach the situation in a more professional manner.

Two days later I was surprised to open the front door to the gaunt image of Robert McCarthy. I recognized him immediately, having met him at Jack's funeral. At the time his quietly spoken words of introduction and his concise and deferential tribute to Jack had impressed me and so made his face memorable, but until the moment I saw him at the door, I had forgotten I had ever met the man.

"Please come in." I stood aside to allow him to pass. I took his cap and coat and noticed his left hand hung limp by his side. I considered for a moment whether to invite him to sit in the kitchen or the drawing room but decided on the drawing room. "How are things at the company?" I asked, indicating one of two straight-backed chairs on either side of a small table. He sat down and I noted how he picked up his limp hand and placed it on his knee.

"Things are very slow, Mrs. Drodge. There is a lot of uncertainty amongst the staff; people are worried about their jobs. There are questions as to who is in charge and about the future. I was asked by the employees to come and see you."

"I'm glad you've come, Mr. McCarthy," I said, looking him straight in the eye. "I had intended calling you this week to set up a meeting. We need to discuss the situation. Perhaps you could show me around the premises and acquaint me with some of the more pressing problems so they can be addressed in a timely manner."

"Yes, of course." He reached to cover a twitch in his limp hand.

Aware that I had noticed, he quickly added. "I would be very pleased to show you around, Mrs. Drodge, at your convenience, of course."

"Very well, I'll see you then at ten o'clock tomorrow morning," I said and stood, knowing that at this juncture there was no more to be said.

For a moment he was at a loss but then coughed softly and said, "Very good, Ma'am."

That was it. As I closed the hall door behind Mr. McCarthy I had a feeling of nervous excitement, of being in control. I had actually taken the first real step towards taking charge of my own plumbing business.

Max followed me around and when he finally got my attention, I said, "Right, I've made up my mind. I'll do it." I then sat down at the kitchen table and began to make a list of the questions I needed to ask Mr. McCarthy.

The following morning, February 4th, 1979, I drove into the yard of James Drodge & Company. I pulled into the reserved parking by the door, parked the car and stepped out. Mr. McCarthy was standing on the top step. He greeted me warmly, opened the door, and I walked in.

The shop, for that was what it appeared to be, was dimly lit and had a dull, musty feeling and the smell of the past. A solid wooden counter to my right wore all the signs of tough, active service over many years. At one time it had been painted brown but that was only evident on parts of the trim that had been spared the abuse of everyday commerce. There was no sign of a cash register. White bathroom fixtures of various sizes and shapes lined the walls. Beside them, stainless steel sinks, both double and single models, stood on their ends against the wall. Higher up on the walls and attached to manufacturers' plaques were several sets of gleaming silver taps. At the back of the room there was a wide archway opening into another room. Beyond that I could see rows of grey metal shelving stacked with brown cardboard boxes labelled in black ink. A wide wooden staircase on my right and towards the back of the shop led to the upstairs and I presumed the office area. There was a newly swept pile of rubbish flanked by a broom and dust pan on the floor by the bottom step.

All of this I took in at my leisure, partly out of interest and partly to give me time to get my breathing under control. The room of course had come to a standstill and all eyes were focused on me. There was a loud flush followed by a deep glug from a well-functioning toilet and the sound of a door opening. A young man appeared from the back. He stopped abruptly and then hurried to stand in front of the pile of rubbish.

"This is Thomas," Mr. McCarthy began, pointing to the man by the rubbish pile. "Thomas keeps the place in order. Sean here is one of our sales assistants, and Mike, our other sales assistant. Where's Mike?" An older man stepped out of the shadows and nodded in my direction. "This is Mrs. Drodge, the new owner of the business."

"I'm glad to finally meet you," I managed to say, "and look forward to working with you all."

We headed up the wide staircase, Mr. McCarthy walking beside me. The silence behind told me that every eye on the shop floor followed us all the way to the top. I was confident of my appearance, having checked every detail carefully before leaving the house and taking particular care that the safety pin at the waist of my skirt was secure.

My office was a large dreary room with a single, dusty window looking onto the yard below. A heavy, wooden desk occupied the middle of the floor with two chairs placed in front and one behind. On top of the desk, neatly stacked, were several beige coloured folders. Other than the folders, it all smelled and looked very dated.

In a nearby office I was introduced to Mavis Nash, queen of accounts receivable, and to Marie Flynn, the excitable invoice clerk who appeared to be amused by the whole business. I'm not sure when I was given the name "Lady Ballcock" by the staff at James Drodge & Company but that day was as good as any. Despite my wish to appear confident and in charge, I felt more out of place than at any other time in my whole life.

In Mr. McCarthy's tiny office I gratefully accepted his offer of coffee and eased into a chair. Marie Flynn, came in carrying a white ceramic mug with the slogan *I love my job. It's the work I don't like* emblazoned in red on the side facing me. She held a tin of Carnation milk aloft. "Milk?" I shook my head. She then dangled a sachet of sugar in front of me. I nodded. She ripped it open and tipped the lot into the mug. "Me too," she said, touching my shoulder companionably. I expect she was referring to the use of sugar, no milk. Mr. McCarthy must have noticed this familiarity, for he immediately said, "That will be all, Marie."

The coffee was strong and bitter but I drank it and was glad of the warmth. Mr. McCarthy passed me a folder containing statements and numbers which I glanced at with vacant eyes and said I wished to take them with me. I then asked, as I had planned, for a thumbnail sketch of his concerns. I later recalled key words like upgrading systems, yellow card filing systems, new product... acrylics, colour, ABS drainage pipes. I allowed him to talk and when he had finished, I was no further ahead and even more bewildered. I drained the last dregs of the coffee from my mug and felt the little pool of sugar at the bottom of the mug trickle down my throat.

He must have sensed my unease, for he said in a kind but not condescending way, "There are copies of these files on your desk. We just need to move ahead slowly. We have good people here with a lot of experience."

I smiled, showing as much confidence as I could muster and decided there and then that I had an ally in Mr. McCarthy. He wanted to make things work. What I did not understand was that he wanted it to work as he saw fit.

"Thank you," I said. "That is good to know." I shook his hand and noted the firm grip and look of assurance in his eyes and wondered what he saw in mine. I promised to get back to him within a few days.

On the way home that day, I drove along the waterfront past Bowring's Department store. The restaurant on the ground floor with its big plate-glass windows looking out onto the harbourfront caught my eye and I decided I was hungry. I swung the car around and turned onto the steep ramp that went straight to the parking lot on the roof of the building. The waitress was busy folding and placing napkins on the tables in preparation for the lunch-time crowd. I took a seat by the window and ordered a glass of red wine and the full special: turkey dinner and apple pie for dessert. She snapped shut the menu and left.

I was tired of myself, I decided, tired of being indecisive and dreary. After lunch, I would go and have a look in ladies fashions. We had a credit arrangement there so I could outfit myself with clothes that at least would fit properly and be somewhat suitable. Then to the shoe department to buy shoes and a bag, and finally I'd have my hair cut and styled.

I did all that and more. I found to my surprise a very charming young woman in ladies fashions who sat me down in a spacious dressing room, normally reserved for bridal fittings, where I could try outfits to my heart's content in comfort and privacy. She had a fine sense of colour and told me I had the perfect figure. I was flattered by her attentions and delighted by my new feeling of buoyancy. "The latest thing in the fashion world is to mix and match," she said, as she displayed various pieces, coordinating colours and replacing skirts with pants, blouses with sweaters, cardigans with smart tailored jackets. She lavished attention on me, going to endless lengths until she felt I was completely satisfied with how I looked. I was used to popping into Brown Thomas on Grafton St. in Dublin or a particular boutique that took my fancy and picking an outfit for an event and departing pleased for the time being. But here I was enjoying myself. I was happy and engaged. Her last idea for my new wardrobe was a lovely camel- hair overcoat with a detachable fox-fur collar. "Very professional, ideal for spring or winter wear, perfect with your colouring," she explained as she unhooked the fur collar. I told her I did not need a coat. "What has need got to do with it? It is made for you, madam, elegant and stylish." We laughed and I bought the coat and charged it all to our credit account with the store. I headed to the hairdresser in fine spirits with no idea as to how I would eventually pay for it all.

That winter I was a woman well-groomed and dressed for business. I had skills, and I was ready to learn about the plumbing business. That mindset alone was a major achievement. I was not always the most agreeable of students, but I quickly came to understand the value of a trusted employee like Mr. McCarthy. He became my mainstay, offering a great deal of practical advice and basic lessons on how the business was run. I liked getting dressed and going to work. I realized very quickly that there was money to be made and I liked being a part of that process.

The work was, in many ways, basic and mundane but to my amazement, at the end of the day, I felt good. I was proud of what I was doing. The anticipation of a challenge was there and a kind of excitement that I could only equate with getting ready for a horse show: endless hours of work and practice, honing skills, grooming and braiding, checking and rechecking that everything was in order.

Things were different in the business environment but the principles were the same: preparedness, attention to detail, knowing your objective. It was beginning to make sense to me. One thing I paid particular attention to was the way in which Mr. McCarthy dealt with the staff and customers. I noted how he consulted with others, how he asked for their opinions and listened attentively to their answers. I noted how they in turn dealt with him, casual yet deferential in their manner. It was not like dealing with the stable hands at Kilgraney. There, one gave orders, made decisions that were not to be questioned. If an opinion was voiced by someone else, it had been asked for or was offered in such a way that it allowed the person in authority to decide.

I have always had difficulty guarding my tongue when meeting and dealing with people. I resolved there and then to be more careful.

Eleanor came by to tell me that she has just been given the job of informing me that the physiotherapist has lodged a complaint regarding my attitude. It seems my attitude is not acceptable. I am to be given lessons in how to behave! That irks me but I cannot be cross with Eleanor. She understands my situation, so I've agreed to be guided by her. Within limits.

There are two things I must address immediately.

1. I must do as I am asked and walk the corridors several times a day and without complaint.

2. I must do, willingly and without argument, the exercises that the physiotherapist has prescribed and make every effort to get on the move.

In addition, Eleanor had her personal recommendation: that I contact the CNIB and talk to them about learning to live with sight loss.

I agreed to items 1 and 2, but my answer to her own suggestion was a firm "No."

She came back a few minutes later with a cup of tea for me. I really must make an effort to be more compliant.

When I told James that I was planning to take over the business, his reaction was positive and he peppered me with praise.

"Good for you, Mother ... excellent ... you'll do a great job ... you'll be good once you get the hang of things ... business woman of the year, coming up."

I was so buoyed by his enthusiasm and often phoned him at school to relate my small successes. Our conversations always ended with, "Does this mean I can stay at private school?" My reply was always non-committal. I had still to find a way to pay his fees.

James at the time was steadily plotting a course for himself. He had plans — big plans for both the long and short term. Being at a private school was integral to the plan. He was studying hard, making connections, learning French and Spanish at school and German on the side from a boy whose family had moved to Quebec temporarily. He wanted to become an accountant and not just any accountant. His plan was to deal in international tax law and fight the big important battles in the accounting world. I could not understand where all this drive and ambition had suddenly come from but it was almost certainly to do with money. It was refreshing and what I wanted to hear.

James had his father's charm. Polite and well spoken, he knew from an early age how to win over even the most troublesome of people. Teachers in particular loved him. He was a winner! He played guitar by ear, much to the delight of his friends. I believe they had a kind of band in someone's basement. I suggested once that he take some lessons.

"Waste of time Mother, I can play well enough. It's not going to further my career."

I thought this a strange thing to say but back then I was more than happy to leave my children to their own devices. They appeared to have a natural sense of independence, could manage without me — or so I thought, until one day, Claire quietly, and without preamble, announced that she and James were like orphans.

At the time I was combing through some catalogues trying to decide on a new line of products. I was only vaguely aware that she was speaking to me and didn't react right away.

"You ignore us, Mummy. Like now. Can you get your head out of those goddamn picture books for one moment and listen to me, or is that too much to ask?"

There was a staggered moment, like the pause before the clock begins to strike the hour. Without looking her way, I said, "That is not an appropriate way to speak to your mother, Claire."

"Mother? You're not a *real* mother."

"So, you want me to join the macaroni and cheese brigade?" I said.

"Yes, as a matter of fact I do."

"Well, I'm afraid that particular formula has not found its way into my book."

She was standing over me. I could see her hands clutching a pile of books to her chest.

"We were always in the way. You just wanted Daddy and now Daddy is gone you still don't want us. Well fine! Who cares!" She turned and ran from the room.

I listened to her progress up the stairs, pounding each tread as if it was being tested for soundness. At the top she paused, then sprinted across the landing to her room. There was a loud thud followed by the sound of splintering wood.

A paralysis crept over me. I felt nothing, no anger, not even relief that she had left the room. What remained was the sound of her voice, quiet and dispassionate, repeating over and over. *You just wanted Daddy and now Daddy is gone you still don't want us.* I sat there for a long time, unable to move. Tears welled up, pooled in the cavity around my eyes, hung on to the rim, and then unable to hold on any longer, quietly dropped over the edge one after the other onto the glossy pages of the catalogue.

Claire had always been a different child, quiet and studious, never consciously seeking attention, but that day she had found her voice and had spoken an awkward truth that forced me to consider what it was I wanted if not my own children. Was I really so callous? I could never bring myself to fully accept that this was true. The problem was I didn't know how to deal with Claire. Her brother was not a problem — he knew how to behave, knew what was expected of him. I couldn't work out what it was that she wanted of me.

Having found her voice, Claire went about establishing her new-found independence. She ignored me at will, often refusing to speak or answer my questions. She was frequently gone from the house, visiting friends, going to movies, studying at the library. She received glowing reports from teachers: the perfect student, well-mannered, polite, outstanding in every way. I often found her report card thrown in a drawer days after it had been sent home. When I commended her on her achievements and tried to make suggestions about her future, she dismissed me out of hand.

"Give it a break, Mummy," was her stock reply.

I resigned myself to the fact that we had nothing to say to each other. Now I think of it, the same could be said about my mother and me. I don't believe I ever had a real conversation with her in my whole life.

As the months went by things were not going too well at work either. My initial enthusiasm had begun to wane. I was just plodding along, the same dust rising and then settling at the end of each day. I doubted myself, constantly feeling unsure and inadequate. I didn't know who I was anymore, what I stood for, what I was doing in that place.

On one particular day I was feeling so lost that I picked up a pencil and began to jot down a list of the things that made me who I was. I was shocked and deeply saddened by the paucity of the list. It turned out to be a meager account of outdated norms, squandered opportunity and a stinging indictment of my very existence. I forced myself to examine the list and think about myself and where I was in life. It was a process that demanded cruel honesty and took strips off my already fragile self. It was embarrassing to read in my own hand what I had thought to be important — but it was therapeutic. Between bouts of tears and pure humiliation, I drew hard, angry lines through words like breeding, position, manners, talent. God help me, I even wrote down *beautiful*. That too got a hard angry stroke. Talent was spared, for I refused to accept that what I could do was worthless, although I was no longer sure. I had reduced my worth to a series of black smudges. I began to giggle half-heartedly. One thing led to another and I added *athletic* to the list. I was an athlete in my day, and I had played the piano very well and as a girl had received certificates of excellence from the Royal Conservatory of Music. Then, in a burst of enthusiasm I added *intelligent* and *educated* to the smudged page. My giggle became reluctant laughter as I added to the foolish list.

Just as I was beginning to feel a little better it occurred to me that my children had not made the list. In fact they hadn't crossed my mind. You must think this very strange, which of course it was. I can admit that now. You see, my lack of maternal instincts was a deep, dark secret that had troubled me for a long time. I had refused to acknowledge its existence.

The day I gave birth to James I knew I was different. When I was nine or ten years old, I had covertly witnessed the birth of a foal and was repulsed and traumatized by the whole experience. I buried it away and told no one. When James was born, it all came surging back, rising like bitter bile to add to my torment. I was no better than the animals in the barn; laid low, down and dirty. The sight of the angry, pink, blood-smeared creature, hanging upside down by his feet at the end of my bed, appalled me. When I was presented with my child, my poor James, the smell turned my stomach and made me vomit. My reaction frightened me and frankly never left me. I thanked God that day that he would never have to experience this humiliation.

I didn't dare share my feelings, just went through the motions and did what was expected of me: accepting compliments on his weight, his size, all the other things people seemed to notice and admire. I watched Jack, breathless with adoration, hold him and never want to let him go. When Claire was born my reaction was even more virulent. To everyone's surprise I didn't even want to hold her. I pretended to be tired.

Claire was right. At that moment I didn't want her. I didn't want children.

In the quiet misery of those long, sleep-interrupted nights, I admitted to myself that I was not cut out for motherhood. This admission was like ice cracking beneath my feet, the freezing water seeping slowly through my flesh and into my bones. It terrified me. I don't know why I felt that way. I couldn't understand, either then or now, how ordinary mothers felt and why they behaved the way they did. Did anyone else in this whole world feel like me? I remember thinking back to an incident that had taken place years before.

I was standing by the main door of a hospital in Dublin waiting for a taxi. A very elegant woman was standing close by. She was beautiful; her skin smooth and golden like the flesh of a ripe peach, but her expression was blank. Her heavy black hair fell around her face in soft waves. She wore a long black mink coat and in her arms she held a newborn baby, swaddled in pink and white. There was a lavish arrangement of flowers on the floor by her feet.

"Your flowers are beautiful," I said.

"My daughter is beautiful," she replied without looking my way.

I wanted to feel different about my children, to find a way to change. How could I speak of such a thing even to Jack? It was impossible. So I remained silent. Not long ago I heard a discussion on the radio on this very topic and women were speaking openly and without reservation, saying they simply did not want children. They cited all kinds of reasons: careers, loss of freedom, poor experience in childhood, even cost was mentioned. But when one woman said, "I just don't feel the need," I wanted to stand up and cheer; she had said what I had wanted to say over all these years of silence. Claire had recognized my limitations.

"We need our mother. You don't want us."

As Claire grew older her presence became a constant in my life. She hovered in the background, silent but watchful. This feeling was, at times, disconcerting but, for the most part, not too bothersome until that particular moment when, like the chick ready to hatch, it all cracked wide open and out it came. "You don't want us."

Claire has never married. When I asked her about this one day, she said, "I haven't met anyone that I love." That didn't surprise me. She seems to go from one relationship to another, constantly on the move. There is no lasting place in her life for anyone but herself — not that I can see.

One evening I went into the drawing room and sat down at the piano. Many times in the past I had considered trying to play again but always shied away. In my youth, piano playing was a serious business: posture, practice, technique. All of this I accepted, understanding the reasons while at the same time anticipating that moment when skill and interpretation come together as one. How I loved that feeling of being swept along as I played, feeling the emotion, creating my own interpretation, making the music my own. As I began to show real promise, the pressure from outside sources to excel stole away the joy. I could no longer find the emotion, or a reason to practice. It became a chore. So I quit.

For Jack, playing the piano was more of a jolly business; banging out the notes music-hall style, singing along with gay abandon, which was what everyone seemed to want. That was how I saw things or wanted to see them. That day when finally I opened the lid and touched the keys, I was surprised when the sound wasn't discordant. I slipped along the seat, my feet automatically reaching for the peddles. One by one the notes rose, simple and sweet and true. My fingers were shy, reluctant to trust the sensation at their tips but I played on, testing myself, searching my memory, picking out arpeggios and progressions and then reluctantly simple fugues and preludes until I was so full of emotion I could no longer continue. I sat there, my eyes glazed, afraid to touch the keys again in case the magic was gone. Over and over again I told myself I could still play, that it was still there, in my fingers, in my heart, in my head, that kernel of pure joy I had once known before the arrival of the grand piano; that quasi-sixteenth-birthday gift with its infernal demands that was supposed to add to the pleasure but instead had spirited it away.

A nudge at my arm and there was Max, looking forlorn and sad. "You thought I was Jack," I said. "You want his jolly, happy music." But he settled down beside me and laid his head on his outstretched paws as if wanting more. I began to play again. This time my fingers found the opening notes of a piece I had great difficulty learning as a student — *Sonatina in A Major*, second movement by Fredrich Kuhlan. It became one of my favourite pieces once I had mastered it. It is a happy, carefree piece, full of delightful trills that reminded me of lambs gamboling about in the fields in the spring of the year. To my great delight, the notes were still there at my fingertips and in my memory, but the playing was laboured. I tried and tried again and Max stayed by me as my fingers worked to do what they had not done in many years. When they ached with weariness, I gave up but I was overjoyed.

I clung tenaciously to this happy place in my life and I resolved to stay focused on this new path of running a plumbing business. Months went by but my struggle continued. I kept my office door closed to give the appearance of being busy. I shuffled statements, order forms, and yellow cards that recorded accounts, all with a blind eye. Mr. McCarthy continued to pour over the task of stock taking and ordering. He was fixated on the new drainage systems and the change in materials being used at the time. I listened as he told me in great detail how the use of cast-iron piping was being replaced with a new material called ABS that was lighter, more cost effective and easier to handle. If we were to service our customers, we needed to place an order as soon as possible to meet the demand. I could hear the urgency in his voice and it unnerved me because I had no idea what he was talking about, nor had I any idea what all this involved.

Drainage systems, dear God, how was I supposed to get excited about drainage systems? In the end, out of sheer exasperation and knowing nothing of what I was doing, I told him to go ahead and order whatever was needed. But the decision caused me concern. I knew I was being foolhardy, that I had made a significant decision without fully understanding what I was doing. This was not acceptable. I had to admit that being there was not enough — I had to find out about drainage systems and the plumbing business or get out.

I had been with the company for close to six months before I held my first meeting with the retail staff. I was shocked to find out that in addition to the two men downstairs who were in retail, we — I — had two other salesmen in my employ. They went about their business on the road five days a week, sometimes more depending on the season. They had been submitting orders and expenses and collecting their commission and I hadn't even known.

I gathered that they worked out of a catalogue, the customer making a decision from a picture and placing an order by number. What was offered was pretty simple. Fixtures were white, the choice of quality limited to low, medium or high. It was fairly steady trade, much of it going to general stores or small hardware stores around the island or to private customers. I was shocked, but did my best to conceal my ignorance and made a note to ask Mr. McCarthy about the terms of their employment.

It was around that time that I received an invitation to a Board of Trade luncheon. The president at that time was a woman and I assumed I had been invited simply to bolster the ranks on the female side, certainly not for my business acumen. Later, I became a member. It was a turning point in business for me. It gave me an opportunity to meet other business people who, at first, I found to be curious about me but in time both helpful and friendly. It was an eye opener and I found the whole process to be both interesting and stimulating. The more frequently I attended, the more relaxed I became, allowing myself to ask questions and learn more about the business climate and the workings of the business community. The women I met were intelligent and highly motivated and worked in all manner of positions, in all kinds of businesses. One in particular was the owner of several hardware stores and a small construction company. She was highly respected and from a good family. I was particularly taken with the president, whom I greatly admired for her assertiveness, knowledge and competence. I was surprised to find out that she was a lawyer by profession and not a business woman. She also was an outsider, like me, but that didn't seem to bother her one iota.

Shortly thereafter she introduced me to a professor from Memorial University's Business Administration Faculty, who had taken a particular interest in the development of small business. He had been the guest speaker at our luncheon. He spoke about the changing business climate in the city, how the influx of money into the province since confederation with Canada in 1949 was steadily changing the face of how business was carried out in the province. He pointed to the demise of local well-established merchants. "The Avalon Mall is just the beginning. The big chain stores," he cautioned, "are moving in and are here to stay. The dangers they pose are significant. Change and move with the times or fail." That was his message.

I came away from there with an idea.

The opening of stores like Canadian Tire and Woolco were having an impact on James Drodge & Company. This had not occurred to me, or, I expect, to Mr. McCarthy. I had dismissed these stores as places where the new-money crowd around town could shop with their baby bonus for shag floor rugs or newfangled house wares, which seemed to be the whole rage, or for car accessories and parts for their new automobiles — but certainly not bathroom fixtures. Nobody else at the luncheon seemed too shocked with this information, but I had not even considered that they were in competition with my company for taps and toilets. Better buying power, no middle man, wider choice of product — these were the buzz words I was hearing. This, it seemed certain, was what was happening. A business scenario was unfolding and a challenge emerging. It was just the beginning.

On my way home I dropped into Canadian Tire and had a good look around. Prior to that, I had never been inside the door. Sure enough, kitchen and bathroom fixtures lined the walls. I noted the prices and the brand names but had no idea how they compared to ours.

A few days later I phoned the professor to ask how I might learn more in terms of how to proceed in my situation. He invited me to attend a panel discussion on this very topic to be held at the university. It was for graduate students but the panel was to be made up of local business people. I could sit in on the discussion and ask questions if I wished. I accepted without hesitation. It was there I learned a little about restructuring and replacing outdated methods of doing business.

That evening I was asked if I would consider accepting a graduate student to do a work term. The student's assignment would be to work within the company for twelve weeks and formulate a plan of action to modernize the administration and workings of the company. The work would be supervised and the report graded. Payment was not obligatory, since work experience was the goal. I would be given a copy of the restructuring plan to implement as I saw fit.

I thought it was an excellent idea.

I was genuinely excited. This was something I understood, something I thought was necessary and of interest to me. With help I could do this. At last I had a purpose.

Mr. McCarthy was not of the same opinion. I recall him standing in the office on the day I told him what was afoot. He was dressed as usual in the navy blue cotton shop coat that he always wore while on the shop floor checking stock and shipments. On his chest, displayed in a neat row like a ribbon bar on a uniform, was an assortment of pens and pencils, well sharpened and in working order. I had observed him on many occasions, his clipboard expertly balanced on his wasted forearm as he counted, checked and rechecked and marked off each item carefully on a delivery sheet.

"Watch out, Mrs. Drodge," he cautioned me, "for the young buck who comes charging through the door, all set to turn the place inside out and then skedaddle off when the damage is done. A lot of damage can be done in twelve weeks."

He continued checking stock as I spoke. "We are looking for fresh, new ideas. He will be very dependent on your experience and knowledge of the business. We must work together and move ahead. We have good, loyal customers. Their loyalty and trust has been forged over thirty or forty years in business. This is not to be squandered."

He was effectively ignoring my concerns. "There is no call for unnecessary aggravation. Loyalty is hard come by these days. Steady as she goes, I say. No need to fix what works."

I could sense trouble looming but I was not to be dissuaded. I called a meeting of all the staff and asked that they cooperate fully with the student, assuring them that when the restructuring plan came in, their opinion would be taken into account at that time. Afterwards I spoke with Mr. McCarthy privately and made it clear that I expected his full cooperation and asked that he make a work space and materials available for the student within the building. I spoke firmly but thoughtfully, aware of my dependence on the man and how important his cooperation was to me.

The student arrived three weeks later, introduced himself as Tim Murray and set to work with all the vigour and enthusiasm of youth. I remember being impressed with his methodical approach and his brisk, open manner. He asked about my main concerns, about the workings of our office, number of employees and client sources. None of which I knew anything about. I called on Mr. McCarthy to provide the answers but I promised myself that never again would I be caught in this situation where I was so ill informed on the workings of my own business. I asked that he keep me advised on a regular basis of his progress.

It was around that time that I first heard one of the men refer to me as Lady Ballcock. I was out of sight but within earshot at the time, so I popped my head around the corner and said, "What a clever title. Quite ingenious!" And it was clever — and very suitable. I told the children about it that evening.

"Perfect," Claire muttered.

James laughed when I told him. "It may not be meant kindly, Mother, but you have taken your best line of defense. Well done!"

There was tension both in the office area and on the floor. The pace of work seemed to have slowed down and in some areas had come to a standstill. Tim Murray had been accommodated in a small windowless room down the hall. There was probably better space available, but I said nothing. I noted on many occasions as I passed Mr. McCarthy's office that Tim was there, sitting on the other side of the desk looking at files and asking questions. Tim was working on a short-term plan. I couldn't quite get a sense of how things were going with Mr. McCarthy until one day, about two weeks after Tim's arrival, I heard raised voices coming from the office.

"I need three pencils, three note pads and three ballpoint pens. Please." The young man's voice was irritated.

"You must return the old pencil stubs and the used pens taped together before I can provide you with more. That is the rule."

"They are not for me; they are for the men on the floor. They are helping me with some statistics and I need them NOW!"

"We do not hand out our supplies without receiving returned —"

"Give me the goddamned pencils so I can get on with my work."

I was about to step into the room when I heard, "Look, Mr. McCarthy, I understand the need to be careful with supplies but I assure you this is necessary. Please, can I have the supplies now and I also need a stapler and a pencil sharpener."

There was a long silence and I heard a chair being pushed back.

I turned to sneak away and heard, "Thank you, Sir, and I apologize for swearing."

A week later he came to me with his short-term plan. That was our starting point. I won't bore you with the detail, but suffice to say our whole system of account keeping, invoicing and ordering needed a complete overhaul. He recommended we do away with our yellow card system, which kept a record of accounts payable and receivable, also all logs of freight etc. and instead he recommended that we outsource our accounts and invoices and in the process save ourselves one thousand dollars per month. To better facilitate all this, we had to make our own barcode and implement it right away. The other major recommendation was that we join a large national buying group, which would provide better buying power for the smaller wholesaler like us.

I was more than happy to find a way of emerging from the depressing, Dickensian atmosphere that surrounded me on a daily basis. This fresh approach placed me firmly at the controls. I was assuming the risk and so the responsibility to insure the transition went smoothly and that it worked.

Those directly involved in the transition were not as enthusiastic. They grumbled about additional work and "at the end of it all getting shafted and replaced by a bloody machine." It went on and on until finally I lost patience.

"If you cannot or will not do the job then I will hire people who can."

I was fighting my own war and if I was to succeed at the business and at the same time keep jobs, I needed help — not moaners. I also was of the opinion that much of the discontent originated in Mr. McCarthy's office and that he was feeling increasingly threatened by Tim Murray. It was therefore incumbent on me to keep a sharp eye on everything that was happening in every department and concentrate on keeping all systems turning over and with a minimum of discord. I had to know and understand clearly what was going on if I wished to be taken seriously. I had to commit to learning about and knowing the business. I needed answers and solutions at my fingertips.

So I went to work. I studied our credit system, identified our preferred customers and problem customers. Balances, to my surprise, were carried by most of our clients and were paid off on a monthly basis but rarely in their entirety. Interest was charged according to a customer's credit rating at anything from two to seven percent: the more reliable the customer, the better the rate.

While all this was going on inside our small shop, outside, excitement was growing. An agreement had been reached to develop the Hibernia oil field off shore. Oil and gas was finally emerging as an industry in Newfoundland. Hopes were high and things were moving as money flowed into the province and well-paying jobs became available. New construction was underway and people were beginning to upgrade and renovate their homes.

Meanwhile, Tim Murray was now hard at work developing a long-term plan for the company. I had become very comfortable with this young man. I liked his approach, his sense of purpose and drive, and his ideas made good sense. He was certainly instrumental in getting me up to scratch. We met frequently to discuss our progress and I discovered that we made a good team. I had no preconceived ideas about the business and how to run it and he was completely up to date on new methods. He also had access to free professional advice. So we forged ahead.

Because we were a small business, we agreed that focusing our efforts on small contractors and their needs and getting individual customers into the store was a good strategy. In addition, individual credit cards from companies like Chargex were being used widely by the individual customer, so that, too, had to be taken into account. It occurred to me the store needed to be more customer friendly. Clients needed to actually see what they were buying and have an alternative to what was available at stores like Canadian Tire and Woolco. It was a risk and would require capital.

Mr. McCarthy took up a position on the sideline and watched as the structure, security and stability of his world was dismantled bit by bit. He became quiet and withdrawn. I knew him to be an intelligent and thoughtful man capable of appreciating and understanding what we were planning. Tim suggested I give him more time to sort through all the proposed changes and gradually move away from old established rules and procedures. He suggested I wait and, when all the plans were in place, that I present Mr. McCarthy with the details and give him the opportunity to judge the benefits for himself.

Something positive was happening and I felt elated. I began to actively seek out new products and discovered from my research that acrylics were the latest in bathroom fixtures. Not only were they lighter and easier to install but they were available in colour. Gold, pink, grey, cream, green, even red was available. Bath tubs were now coming in with a fancy surround that gave a new clean look to the tubs, vanities with drawers and cupboards, and all manner of new-style faucets and shower fixtures were available — especially in the more upscale lines.

There were trade shows to attend in Toronto and Montreal where I saw whirlpool tubs and hot tubs for the first time. Attending them was a way to make more informed decisions on what to buy and what to disregard. I was confident this was the way to go. I have to admit, it was a gut feeling as opposed to a sound business decision but Tim Murray was in full agreement and his supervisor seemed happy with the plan and that was enough to drive me forward. Everything appeared to be going along well.

The office staff had taken a liking to young Tim, particularly young Alice Neary who, having discovered he had a sweet tooth, had taken to bringing him sweet treats on a regular basis. I secretly hoped that was all she was offering. I needed him on task. They were also dealing well with the restructuring process. The retail staff was delighted with the idea of new products and a new showroom to show them off. One of them took an order from a very well-known and important client for a red, heart-shaped whirlool bathtub. Unfortunately the very exalted client never saw fit to pay the bill.

The new drainage systems had arrived. Aware that this was the one area in which Mr. McCarthy had taken an interest, I waded across the muddy yard one day to take a look at the new stock and assess a perceived problem with storage. I shivered in the cold as he explained with great care and in detail the nature of the materials.

"They are so lightweight," he said "even you could assemble them."

He was carefully fitting two pieces together as he spoke and when they were securely joined and tested smartly with a quick tug, he held them out for me to do the same. I hesitated but gave them a serious twist. "Excellent, good decision," I said handing them back.

"However," he pressed on, "they can be removed very easily and quietly from the premises." He passed the specimen from hand to hand and eye-balled me, just in case I hadn't been paying attention. "New metal doors with secure locks are needed on the sheds. Otherwise we are wide open to theft."

I had noticed on the way in how the door was propped open with a length of wood, so I assured him I was aware of the problem and that replacement was in our long-term plan. A week later, a third of our first shipment disappeared overnight and was never recovered. The long term quickly became the short term. I ordered new doors, had a security system installed and reminded myself to listen, in future, to those who knew better.

I turned my attention to expenditures. I needed approval of the plan and funding to carry it out. I set up a meeting with the accountant who had been dealing with the business for years. The cash from Jack's insurance was running out rapidly and I was beginning to spend money

I simply did not have. Tim was already working on a budget and suggested that I wait until this was ready before going to see my accountant. We worked day and night on the project, getting estimates, identifying objectives and priorities and finally coming up with a bottom line on cost and estimated revenues. I was very impressed with the finished plan, although frightened when I saw the final figures on the cost of the project. It was something I wasn't quite prepared for. Fear began to crawl around inside me and gnaw at my confidence. It was Tim once again with the buoyancy of youth who urged me on and told me that I must try. I had to move forward, even if I fail.

"Failure is not an option, Tim."

"Good. Then we must succeed."

That evening, I was strangely energetic. I went over the plan again and again. I walked the floor, phoned James at school for his advice, only to realize once again that his only concern was whether or not he could now stay on at school in Quebec. I even tried to engage Claire in conversation, but she told me that she had a test the next day and had to study. I heard Fred come in and I called out to him. I hadn't spoken with Fred in several weeks and it was strangely unsettling to see him come up from the basement. I wondered again about his position in our house. Calling out to him had been a natural reaction. I needed someone to talk to, yet now that he was there standing at the top of the stairs I was at a loss for words and not even sure what it was I wanted to say or why I had called out. There followed an awkward silence when we just looked at each other. Then he said, "I expect you want me to leave."

"No, no, not at all, that was not on my mind. I just need to talk to someone."

He nodded. I indicated a chair at the table. He took the last step slowly and then seemed to hold his ground.

"Sit down — please," I said. I didn't know where to begin, but the conversation went something like this: "I have taken over the Drodge family business. It is very run down and in need of restructuring."

He looked at me in that disconcerting way of his, but said nothing.

"In fact I am eager, very eager, to get on with the project."

"That's good."

"I have worked on a plan, as to how it can be done, but —"

"But?"

"It is a big commitment."

Say something, man, anything to encourage me. But he remained silent.

"I am concerned that I am being foolhardy. I will have to borrow a sizable amount of money."

"That is a legitimate concern. Not to be concerned would indeed be foolhardy."

"It will be difficult."

"All the better."

There was a kind of bleak wisdom in his terse words that made me cringe a little and shy away. I was no longer sure what to say or if I wanted to take the conversation any further. Then he stood up and said, "Find your true strength, Sylvia. Find it … and don't be afraid."

Did I imagine it, a faint lilt in his voice? I'm not sure but I see, in my mind's eye, Fred, smiling — he is standing by the piano and Jack is playing alongside, both full of song and not a care in the world. *Don't be afraid of the dark.*

I decided that night that Jack was with me. He was there urging me to go ahead.

I went to bed happy. The last and final chat on the matter was with Max. This time I was telling, not asking. "I have a fierce natural urge to win," I told him. "The tougher the competition, the greater my resolve; horse and rider must find their oneness. It is time to hit stride. There is only one goal now, to win. I will do it and it will work." He hopped on the bed without invitation and settled down.

I think of this moment of decision now and it warms my wretched heart and reminds me of the times in my life when I glowed with pride and determination; when I revelled in my considerable ability to take on a challenge and succeed. I am wondering now, as I mull over all this in my mind, if I can once again muster up enough courage and determination to find a way. Could I possibly find the energy and the will to climb out of this rut and again make a life for myself? I have allowed myself to grow old before my time. Like an old turtle I want to retreat into the dark security of my shell and hide.

When I walked through the door of the small accounting firm of Peter Penny & Associates, I had assumed the role of confident, aggressive business woman. Things had been carefully researched and I had at least a fair knowledge of the business. Plan in hand, I knew what I wanted. I had not anticipated dealing with a very elderly man seated behind a desk littered with an assortment of papers.

"I went to school with James Drodge senior," he said as he shook my hand. "I have served as accountant to the company for fifty-eight years. We played hockey together with…" He rubbed his forehead as if searching for a word or a name, gave up and then began to study my business plan, muttering to himself, occasionally drawing back to better accommodate his eyes. Every so often he jotted notes and figures on a legal pad. When he finally lay the pen down and looked up his gaze was unwavering.

"This is a big undertaking for a woman," he said, "for any woman, never mind one of your background and limited experience. You may fail."

"You may fail." His first words of professional advice reached me on a single breath! I looked at that long, sagging face with its two big, watery eyes brimming with what seemed to be unshed tears and a lower lip that hung down, showing off his long teeth and receding gum line.

If I had a mind to fail do you think I'd be here, you silly fool. This is 1983… Instead I said, "I do not intend to fail, Mr. Penny. I intend to succeed."

He cleared his throat and proceeded to dissect the plan with surprising clarity. He was talking money, cash flow, past earnings, increased sales, better profitability, projected earnings, credit balances. I was taken aback at the how much he had absorbed on a single reading.

"A very commendable effort, my dear. However, you are a woman, venturing into a man's world without a tad of experience."

"I studied commerce," I said, ignoring the curl of a smile lurking at the corners of his mouth, "and just about ran the family stud farm for several years in Ireland."

"Yes, as I say, all very commendable, my dear, but this is not of help in your situation."

I was beginning to feel that I was being scolded by another version of my father, one just as infernally condescending and authoritative. One who does not like his opinion to be questioned.

"My situation?"

"This is a plumbing business, Mrs. Drodge, not a fashion boutique." Another smile.

I was no longer anybody's fool. I understood exactly what he was saying. A year earlier, I might have agreed. I lowered my head and pretended to look chastened, giving him a few moments to relish his perceived victory. Then I fired back. "Are you suggesting, Mr. Penny, that because I am a woman, I am therefore unable to run this business."

"I am telling you that before you ever get a chance to try running this business, you will be unable to borrow the money necessary to do so."

"Because I am a woman?"

He sighed. "Banks are reluctant to lend money unless they are sure of returns."

"I am neither a fool nor a pauper," I said. "I own a business and a house, I also have some collateral in the bank. Not only am I capable of learning, I must learn." I struggled to control a tremor in my voice but I forced myself to eyeball him.

He shook his head. "I understand your position, Mrs. Drodge, but I'm afraid it won't work. I'm sorry, my dear, but that is reality."

If you call me *dear* one more time, I thought, I'll plant my posterior right on your desk, look you straight in the eye and tell you very directly that *I am not 'your dear' and that if call me that one more time…*

Instead I pulled on my gloves very slowly and deliberately and stood before he had a chance to end the conversation.

"Good day, Mr. Penny." I smiled. "I am sure you have the best interests of the company at heart and I shall give your advice some thought."

I was out of the door and into my car before he had time to draw breath. I left there, more determined than ever to make the plan work.

I called James that evening and told him that he would be coming home for good at the end of term.

The Board of Trade luncheon was scheduled for the following day. I needed to consult with some of the people there. I was not totally surprised my gender was an issue, but to be the main stumbling block in my path to revamping the business was not acceptable.

I spoke first with the president, Angela Fowler. She agreed that being a woman in business made life more difficult at times, but she added, "Don't forget, women manage on a daily basis, men learn to manage." She laughed. "One piece of advice though: do your homework thoroughly and be prepared for rejection. Go to every bank and credit union manager in the city and if that fails, there are other options we can discuss. Listen carefully and make your decisions based on the best advice you can get. It will be a fight, Sylvia, but go carefully. It's not smart to be too smart." She looked at me intently to be sure I understood.

Angela and I became friends in the years to come, seeing each other at business functions and sometimes socially. Many times in my business life her advice stood me in good stead. Through her I became a part of a very helpful network of both women and men who were interested and supportive of women in business. When I retired I lost contact with Angela and my colleagues in the business world. I have never been good at either making or holding on to friends. There always had to be a reason for me to pay attention to someone. I suppose I used people happily until I no longer needed them. Angela was such a wonderful person.

As predicted, it was indeed a battle to find the money. I went from one financial institution to another, starting with Mr. Holmes. I got to know intimately what in the banking world was called *THE FOUR Ms*: markets, materials, money, and management. With practice I became adept at finding my way through the maze of questions and answers. I was grilled on facts and figures, which I quickly learned to have at my fingertips.

I was no longer shy at marketing my own strengths. I was passionate about the fact that I had a vision for the business, that I had carefully identified our markets, could see in our growing economy where new markets were developing and what people wanted. I was convinced the people working at the shop were for the most part sound and that, in spite of the fact that the company had been virtually leaderless for several years, it was still profitable. It spoke to the experience and skill of the ground crew. We had already begun to upgrade our stock to meet demands and there was no significant backlog of stock in warehouses.

My own situation as manager was evidently the weak link and this, together with the fact that I had no husband to sign a loan, was what it all came down to in the end. That was the bottom line. I went from one bank to the next, then the credit union, which to give them their due were more encouraging and respectful but, in the end, the answer was no.

Mr. Holmes was the one who in the end helped me to find a way. He convinced me that if I wanted to go ahead with my plans, my best choice was to use my house as collateral and use the money raised as share capital. He explained that seventy-five percent of the value of the house would be in shares — that there would be quarterly dividends — but I risked losing the house if the business was not profitable, since the bank would have to be paid by the sale of the house. At that time, I would retain twenty-five percent of the value of the sale and any residual monies after the bank had been paid.

I was reluctant to make myself even more vulnerable. Numbers, and dollar signs, coupled with a healthy dose of fear muddled my brain. I was close to panic.

"Mrs. Drodge." He waited for my attention and I thought, he knows I am beginning to panic. "You have a sound business plan and an admirable commitment. I feel confident that there is a fairly good chance of success for this venture. The bank does not take a risk like this lightly."

"The risk is mine, not yours," I managed to get out.

"Banks do not like the idea of foreclosure. We are taking a calculated risk, Mrs. Drodge. I am willing to take a chance on this one succeeding."

Having secured the financing and set things in motion, my next instinct was to let Mr. McCarthy go but, on second thought, I remembered that I was the weak link in the plan. I had little knowledge of the plumbing business, particularly the practical side, and he did. I had to acknowledge he was a good worker but one who held on to the past like a secure lifeline. He was intelligent, so perhaps, as Tim had suggested, given time to work through the plan on his own he might come around to my way of thinking and become an asset. I arranged a meeting with him in my office.

He was a punctual man so at precisely the appointed time he knocked and entered, closing the door quietly behind him. I had placed a chair close to my desk.

"Please take a seat."

"I would rather stand if you don't mind."

I shot him a glance, not quite sure how to respond. "Please," I said, "I have something important to discuss with you." I indicated the chair again.

He took the chair reluctantly.

I thought I should begin on a positive note. "Your job has not been easy for the past few years," I began. "You have basically been left to run the business with no help or guidance from the family. You have managed to keep us solvent, even to turn a small profit. I want to acknowledge your contribution and thank you for that."

He nodded.

"If we are to continue in the business we must continue to make changes." I watched him, carefully hoping to be guided by his response. "I plan to upgrade our stock and cater to a more affluent clientele. I intend to convert some of the upstairs area here into a high-end showroom where our customers can come, feel comfortable and get advice on renovating their bathrooms. They will be able to actually see and handle the new products that are available."

All this time he was focused on a point just over my right shoulder as if what I was saying was of no importance to him. "Mr. McCarthy," I pressed on, "I want to have a team approach to this project, the sales people, the buyer, the accounts department, management, all working together. I want you to consider heading up the team. That is the plan. I have here a file with all the current information, catalogues, data, a floor plan for the showroom. I want you to take it away with you, take your time, think about it and let me know within the next few days if you are willing to work on this project. Plumbing supplies will continue to be your responsibility. Your advice on supplying PVC materials was excellent. Just the kind of forward thinking we need." I reached across the desk and placed the file in front of him. "Shall we say Friday for a decision?"

I related the whole conversation to Max later on. I was proud of myself. I was learning.

Friday came and Mr. McCarthy returned to my office in a more positive mood than I expected. He had done some research on his own and found that my plans for the new showrooms were sound and that one of our competing companies already had a small showroom.

It was an exciting time for me. We were moving forward, images of how the showroom would look, choosing which products to stock, shedding some of our baggage from the past. Bathrooms were no longer just for utility purposes. They were bright and inviting places to relax. Hardware was being marketed as a distinctive accent. Brand names were displayed prominently and to the discerning eye the product spoke of quality and good taste and money. The marketing plan was to bring the customer's attention to these details. I set about staging two modern-style bathrooms in the store that would simulate a home situation and be complete with lighting and accessories, the idea being to make the customer imagine their own situation and see what was possible. At James Drodge and Company, quality, style and comfort were to be the selling points.

I have to admit it was a bit of a stretch of the imagination to think of upscale bathrooms right in the middle of our dingy plumbing supplies shop but I went ahead, finalized the plans and set about controlling the implementation. I arranged a meeting with the team. Every employee was invited to attend, right down to Tom the cleaner and the men in the yard. I outlined the changes to be made and had a detailed job description for each employee. I placed emphasis on order and cleanliness both inside and outside, pointing out that once the wooden floors were sanded and refinished and the paintwork redone there would be zero tolerance for slovenly untidy work spaces. There was a lot of reorganization to be done and I looked for everyone's cooperation. For now, the ground floor would remain the same, cleaner and brighter but geared to service. The top floor was to reflect the upscale environment. I learned later that this cleanout became known amongst the staff as *The Royal Flush*. I set a time frame of two months to have the new plan in place. The sales team, headed by Mr. McCarthy in consultation with me, would choose and place orders for new stock and present a budget. I would personally oversee the renovations.

And so we set out on our new venture. Sean, the young salesman whose territory was mostly outside, couldn't have cared less about rules and past procedures. He wanted to sell, sell, sell and make money. His approach was informal and persuasive. He wanted quick decisive answers and speedy service. He was a dynamic salesman and understood his particular clientele.

Mike, who dealt with local businesses, liked to consult with his clients and help solve their particular problems. He asked contractors for plans and budgets, thereby encouraging thoughtful planning. He was also aware that once a customer left the shop, getting them back in was not easy. He was careful when recommending colour and consulted with the homeowner before a final decision was made. He frequently came to me seeking "a woman's perspective." It was interesting to see how different people functioned in different ways. As we began to grow and take shape I came to understand that the salesmen were the key to my success.

Sean was expanding his territory across the island. And his expenses were growing accordingly. I came to realize there were boom times and slow times in sales, especially in the small rural communities. Before Christmas and spring were boom times. I decided to offer him a bi-weekly base salary together with his commission and to cut out expense claims. The base salary helped during slow times and encouraged him to spend carefully.

Thomas's work hours were changed from all day to two mornings and three evenings a week. Main cleaning was to be done after hours.

These were the first changes and as time went on and need arose, there were more. Tim Murray finished his work term. I gave him a glowing report and a cheque for two hundred and fifty dollars. He'd earned it. We were both pleased.

A new sense of confidence was creeping into my life, urging me to explore new ideas and take chances. Adjustment at times was difficult but my two years of commerce education turned out to be invaluable. I had mastered the skill of reading a financial statement and balance sheet, and understood the importance of cash flow to a business. Those first few years, I worked from early morning and often late into the night. In the evenings, Max was my constant companion. Wherever I was, he was there, tucked in beside me. The bed was his favourite spot and mine too. I was obsessed with checking and rechecking the books, watching for credit problems, controlling the flow of stock in and out of the building, assessing the success or failure of particular initiatives. Just trying to keep everyone happy, including myself, was a challenge. I fretted constantly — even when things were going well.

Jack was often in my thoughts then. In the middle of the upheaval I sometimes took a moment to wonder what Jack would think; his Sylvia, surrounded by toilets and sinks, mired in the dust and dirt of the past, trying to find a way to make it all work. Gone were the days when my challenges were dealing with basic tasks: how to sew a button on a shirt, mend a ripped hem. To Jack, my incompetence in those areas was amusing, even attractive. Sometimes I thought so too and played along, like when I tried plucking and cleaning my first partridge. I ended up with feathers in my hair, on my clothes, on the floor. But I became adept at the job.

On the night we met, perhaps Jack recognized the tough, fiercely persistent side of my nature. What was it about me that put him in mind of Grace O'Malley? Bald or not, she was, without doubt, a striking and remarkable woman: she who commanded her fleet of merchant ships; she who fought savagely to maintain her position in the man's world of commerce in sixteenth century Ireland; she who thought nothing of challenging the might of Queen Elizabeth I of England; she who won her battle for fair play and the great queen's admiration. Had he recognized another bitch of a business woman or just a tall striking woman?

As I lay in bed pondering all this, I sat bolt upright and with a fierce determination I told him, "I will emulate her, Jack, and when I succeed I will be more than an ornament. You know what they call me, Jack? They call me Lady Ballcock. I like it, Jack. It rings a powerful chime in my ear."

Throughout our married life it became increasingly evident that here was a major faultline in the relationship between Jack and me. Sometimes he treated me like an unusual and exotic specimen, a kind of trophy brought back from his travels abroad. He never got to know my world beyond that one disastrous visit to Kilgraney. He never fully understood that my life was built on the trappings of wealth and position. Take them away and I was deprived of my source of energy. I was unable to move ahead.

Jack knew every inch of my body but so little of the world within. I never got to show him my exceptional ability and skill when riding a beautiful thoroughbred. Never got to show him the trophies and ribbons I was so proud of, never played the piano for him. I know I didn't assert myself, that I sat back and watched his life progress as he wished, and allowed mine to slip away. It had to do with the fear, fear of widening the gap between us, fear that it would make the situation more difficult than it already was and fear of losing him altogether. You see, I had nowhere to go. My pride would never allow me to go back to my father "with my two bastards in tow."

"Father, forgive me, I have sinned against heaven and before thee. I am not worthy...." Never! I believed then that I loved and needed Jack more than he loved or needed me. Sometimes I wonder if I knew how to love Jack, if I understood his needs, cared enough for him. I don't recall anyone ever truly caring for me, so how could I know how to care for others? Even Granny's love, which I cherished most of all, depended on me being "a Bolfe through and through." I was willing to go along with her game so we understood each other and got along well. Whatever it was that Jack and I had back then, I doubt now that it would have seen us happily into old age.

When things were finally set up and going well at James Drodge & Company, I made the decision to put most of the profits back into the business and to use the remainder to supplement what was left of the insurance for our household expenses. We were on a strict budget. James had settled in at school here and seemed happy enough to be back with his friends. Like the rest of us, he had to make do. I was glad to have him back. His presence had always been a source of activity and joy around the house.

Claire, too, had perked up somewhat. Having him back seemed to settle her down. She was constantly on the lookout for him as if much depended on his being there. She even paid attention when he told her that she looked scruffy. The house took on a different air. When I came home in the evening, there were shoes in the hallway, sports equipment lying around, noise and smells of cooking. I learned to ignore the mess and live with the change. I had more important things to worry about. James wanted to join the tennis club that summer and it seemed like a good way to keep him occupied in a place where he could meet the right kind of friends. Claire wasn't interested.

That summer, to relieve my stress, I began playing the piano again. I played with abandon, tripping over the half-forgotten notes, faltering constantly. I knew in my heart I would never again play like I did as a girl. The flexibility in my fingers was not there anymore but I pressed on. I delved into Jack's collection of popular music and began to pick out the familiar melodies and found myself humming along as I played. I could still sight read and picked up the rhythms and notes quickly. I was enjoying myself, knowing that there was no one there looking over my shoulder, ready to pounce when I made a mistake. It didn't matter anymore. I alone set the parameters for what was acceptable. Claire surprised me one evening when she presented me with two books of music she had bought with her own money.

"You can change them if they are not what you want," she said casually, laying them on top of the piano and turning to leave.

She had chosen well: *The Well-Tempered Clavier* books 1 & 2. They were the same books I had used as a young woman. I was touched that she cared enough to seek out them out, so to show my appreciation, I went at these familiar pieces again with renewed enthusiasm, not caring if I missed a note or held it too long.

One evening, shortly after James had returned home from Quebec, I had just finished playing a Shubert sonata. I must have played particularly well that evening because I felt unusually pleased and quite emotional. I sat there quietly feeling the music settle inside of me. A slight movement behind me made me turn. It was James.

"I didn't know you could play like that, Mom. You're good!" He had begun to call me Mom after he returned from school.

"I played when I was a girl, but I lost interest."

"Did Dad know?"

I shrugged. "It wasn't his kind of music. Besides I had grown to — never mind. I didn't want to play."

"But, you play very well."

"Thank you, darling. I just like to play for myself. It helps me."

I escaped then, saying I had some work to do.

As luck would have it, we hit a prosperous time in business. There were signs everywhere that the economy was picking up. The barcode system had been installed and we had simplified our buying system and accounting process. New stock was arriving on a regular basis and our first renovations were completed.

"It's like steppin' through the looking glass," Alice, the young invoice clerk, exclaimed on seeing the finished showrooms. "You should have a grand opening and let everyone see. They'll never believe you can get all this here in St. John's. It's right beautiful. They go mad around here to fix up the house for Christmas. Lots of people would love to see this."

A Grand Opening! I chose an evening in late September for the event. I compiled a list of customers and prospective clients and invited them to a wine and cheese reception and grand opening. I also sent invitations to the local newspapers. It was yet another risk, and one which made Mr. McCarthy shake his head.

"We don't do that kind of thing in the plumbing business. Not here," he told me.

"Then it's a good reason to start. We must get people into the shop and talking about our stock. So best bib and tucker and tell the others the same. I particularly want the sales people here."

Thirty-two people came. Alice had taken ownership of the idea and set about counting each head as they arrived. Together with the staff, it looked like a fair crowd.

It created a buzz in certain quarters. One reporter came early and interviewed me. She also took photographs of the showroom and was particularly taken with the pale green and cream décor with the brass accents in one. Two days later, there in *The Evening Telegram* was our new showroom looking really splendid and a headline: *James Drodge Gets a Face Lift*. It was just what I wanted. At the board of trade luncheon several people mentioned the article and came to congratulate me. We were off to a good start. By Christmas our sales in bathroom fittings had tripled.

I came in one evening quite late and there was a brown package on the kitchen table addressed to me. I picked it up, scrutinizing it as I went up the stairs to bed, Max hot at my heels. I looked in on the children. Claire was reading, James was working on an English essay. "There's a package for you." He spoke without looking up. Claire only grunted when I wished her good night.

I was limp with exhaustion, happy in a vague sort of way with the distraction of an unexpected package and hoping it had nothing to do with plumbing supplies. I saved opening it for later, for that heavenly moment when I found the comfort of my bed. Max climbed up beside me and assumed his usual position, keeping watch until I settled. I took my time undoing the rough string and stiff brown paper. It had been a while since I had received an unexpected gift, if indeed it was a gift.

Guilt leaves an indelible imprint. I recognized immediately the grey blue folder. The realization sent a spasm through my exhausted body. All I could think was, he knew; Fred knew I had been snooping in his room. Max jumped up in alarm, his paws trampling the bed cover. I grabbed the discarded brown paper, the string, a sheet of folded white paper that now lay on the bed. It was all part of the evidence, part of my shame.

In my haste, the folder slipped from my fingers. The drawings slipped out and fanned like a deck of cards onto the quilt. A worried paw landed smack on the grey-blue cover.

"Get down." I pushed the poor creature aside. Max jumped off the bed and stood back at a respectable distance. A whimper sounded from the back of his throat.

I picked up the drawings one by one, carefully and methodically placing the protective sheets of tissue between each one and returned them to the folder. When I was sure they were safe I reached for the sheet of white paper. It was a hand-written note.

I have read it many, many times in the past, so I will try to remember his exact words. He wrote: *These drawings were done with respect and admiration and are not intended to be disparaging in any way, but rather to show the dignity of the individual in times of joy, stress, heartache, confusion, regret — the emotions that shape our daily lives.* Then he goes on to say, *As you can see, Sylvia, you are the source of my inspiration. Forgive me if you feel that I have used your image inappropriately and without your permission. Let me simply say that I was compelled to record what I observed at the time.* He went on to thank me for having allowed him to stay downstairs for so many years and that he felt it was time for him to move on.

Then he wrote: *These drawings are yours to do with as you wish. I hope you will understand. If I were to draw you now I know I would portray a woman of courage and determination. I saw that spark in your eyes the night we spoke about your decision and I knew you had found a new direction in life. One day I hope to find the same for myself.*

He wished me success in my business and said I had been an inspiration to him. Imagine! It was signed, *With admiration, Fred.*

I don't know if I can fully explain to you the impact these drawings had on me. When I first saw them, I saw myself as painfully exposed and that, in itself, was disturbing. My response to each sketch was purely emotional but in time, as I developed the ability to put distance between me and the sketches, I came to appreciate not only the depth and range of the feelings they evoked, but also the skill of the artist and the sweep of his imagination.

I have studied them over and over again, frequently finding small but meaningful details that had previously escaped my eye. I recall particularly the one entitled *Distraught* — the bleakness of that pen and ink image of the woman's head and neck, the face partly in shadow and the eyes leaping off the page, animal like, defiant, daring a predator to approach, is very disturbing. But it is the curve of the full, bottom lip expertly caught in the light, giving the face a distinct hint of vulnerability, that I find most fascinating.

The piece, *Pastels on Paper*, is quite different. An elegant woman, draped in the trappings of a glamorous world is seated on a straight-backed chair smoking a cigarette. She is looking at the world around her through a haze of smoke. In the background are people, loosely sketched yet recognizable, particular features exaggerated for comic effect. The expressions are striking: a mean curl at the corner of a mouth, a wiry eyebrow arched in amusement, a nose flared in mock anger.

I wish I knew what became of Fred. I have come to acknowledge and even appreciate many of the good qualities that Jack had so often pointed out to me but which I had refused to see. I have made some inquiries but he is not in St. John's, of that I am sure. One day I hope to return the sketch pad to Fred along with an apology for invading his privacy.

It would be lovely to hear him sing again. He really did have a fine voice.

It was Lady Ballcock and not Sylvia Bolfe-Carter who finally managed to receive an invitation to Government House. In the old days I would have been delighted; now it amused me. I had moved on and had more important things to be concerned with. However, an invitation like this still carried a certain cachet.

So when the crested envelope arrived with an invitation for cocktails aboard the Royal Yacht Britannia to meet with His Royal Highnesses,

Prince Charles and Princess Diana, I was surprised. When I mentioned the invitation to Angela, she told me that she too had been invited. "These days women in business get attention. Particularly women like you who are breaking new ground. You are making waves, my dear." At last, in this new world, I was a person of note! A plumbing guru!

On the appointed day, I wore what was still the best dress in my closet, a silk chiffon designer dress, a remnant of the past. The fabric was a fiery coral, handpainted with splotches of turquoise, cream, yellow and deep blue. It matched my mood perfectly. With appropriate alterations and some updating it also matched my budget. I placed Granny Bolfe's pearls at my throat. When I looked in the mirror I saw an open and confident woman, only a trace of the old haughtiness still evident in her demeanor.

"Meet Sylvia, Lady Ballcock, Granny," I quipped.

I enjoyed that event. I was relaxed and happy and at ease in the company. People approached me quite naturally to make conversation which was pleasant. I met several new and interesting people from different walks of life, all apparently successful or on the up and up. There were also faces from the past; people whose company I had at one time coveted. One such couple, from the old St. John's elite and whom I had met years ago at some function or other, came to join our group. The husband, a jolly, blustery sort of fellow, nodded in my direction and in a loud voice said, "Sylvia, my dear, you look marvelous. Very elegant!"

I smiled and thanked him. His wife, wearing a puffy pink dress that was a little too tight and a little too young for her years, claimed his arm.

"I remember that dress from years ago," She said. "Longer then, or am I mistaken?"

I allowed my gaze to momentarily sweep over her and then, without acknowledgement, turned my attention back to her husband. The fuchsia mouth was still working.

"I hear the business is doing well, Sylvia. You've remodeled, I hear?"

"It was a good business to begin with but a little updating is always interesting."

"Wish I could say the same for mine. We should have a chat one of these days — share your secret."

I was aware that his retail business on Water Street, which had been in the family for several generations, was about to follow several others and close its doors. I smiled and said, "Yes, I've had some excellent advice which I'd be happy to share with you."

The conversation found a new route. Someone mentioned the previous Royal Visit in '67.

"Very nice, very nice," our jolly fellow said. "The Queen Mum that time, I believe."

"Yes, she came in '67 for the hundredth anniversary of Confederation," somebody offered. "That was the occasion when a cross section of society was invited to Government House to meet Her Majesty. What a carry on that was."

Mr. Somebody then went on to tell everyone how invitations to the event were distributed to all manner of political hacks and cronies, who showed up in their rented suits and clip-on bow ties.

"There were words exchanged on that occasion between the premier and the lieutenant governor. Almost came to fisty cuffs," Jolly said, "but the *little prick* couldn't reach. That's what saved His Honour. Ha, ha!"

The banter continued, followed by bursts of laughter. Looking around me that day I could only reflect on how things had changed around St. John's since I had come here as a young woman. The starch had been eliminated from society just as it had from the gentlemen's collars.

I decided it was time to go. I'd had enough. I passed my glass to the waiter and went to join the receiving line to meet the royal couple.

When it came my turn to shake Princess Diana's hand, I recall being pleasantly aware that we were at the same eye level, looking directly into each other's eyes. A moment followed when we regarded each other more carefully than was usual or appropriate, a moment when our handshake lasted just a little longer than was called for. It was a brief but tacit connection, something that went beyond formal politeness. I sensed a spark of interest that, under different circumstances, might have initiated a conversation. In that brief exchange I recognized in her lovely eyes complete boredom.

Like the repeating bars of a song, the details of that event stayed with me. At the end of the day, one had to wonder what all the fuss was about; a pretty girl and her pompous husband, both of whom appeared jaded by the whole charade. It made me think back to my own past and see it for what it truly was, fool's gold, glitter without substance. My present situation was something I was proud of. Running a business had empowered me. I had developed new skills: clear vision, purpose, expertise. Marketing, I had discovered, was a skill to be learned and good marketing had real and tangible results.

Dealing with numbers was not my favourite side of the business, but it was the one that needed careful scrutiny if I was to succeed. So I pushed ahead, taking every opportunity to meet and cultivate people who could help me in any way. I worked at it diligently, networking with contractors and the professional decorators who were beginning to set up shop in the city. I fought for contracts; I scoured design books for new products and ideas and then travelled to shows in Toronto, Montreal and later New York to buy these products. Often, I found myself in over my head or in tricky situations, but I always found ways to either charm or wiggle my way out. I resolutely stood my ground, even resorted to the old trick of bullying when necessary. I refused to be dismissed or brushed aside. Lady Ballcock was getting a reputation as a hard-nosed business woman. I embraced the title with measured humour. It suited me just fine. There were those who said *Brava* and there were those who referred to me and my aggressive style in unflattering ways, but the truth was, I was being noticed in business circles.

My children were faring just fine during this period. For several years things were pretty lean. I worked at the business and they ran the household. A certain amount of cash was allocated each week so they had to be careful not to overspend. This may sound rigid but it was the only way I knew how to make ends meet. They learned to cook as I had done from *Mrs. Beaton*, and took turns doing so. They also shared household chores. It was difficult to begin with and there were rows over division of labour but once we got into a rhythm, things went fairly smoothly.

Claire was inclined to dodge her duties and rely on James to pick up the slack. I left that for them to sort out. Exam time, never before an issue, suddenly became something we all dreaded. Claire's marks were still very good but the possibility of big scholarships envisaged by her teachers seemed less likely. I tried to talk with her about this one day but having a conversation from the other side of a closed door was impossible. Other than her taste in music, which was eclectic, she had few interests outside of academics. On one of the rare occasions that I was invited into her room, I asked about her friends.

"I see them at school," she said

"And after school?"

"Mummy, give it up, they do stuff that I'm not interested in."

"Not stuff, dear, activities. Do watch how you speak."

"Mummy, I'm not interested. Leave me alone."

This was typical. She had become a law unto herself. I consoled myself with the fact that she was home and not gallivanting around town or at the Avalon Mall, which I gathered was the latest haunt for the young people.

Although James and Claire got along well, they were very different. James liked school and did very well but Claire was exceptional. Often when I came home in the evenings, I'd hear them in Claire's room, music blaring from behind the closed door. James lived for sports — tennis, soccer — and eventually had a summer job teaching tennis to little children. On one occasion as I drove by Bannerman Park, I saw him there with Fred, looking as if they were practicing soccer. I asked him about this later.

"Fred has offered to coach me. He tells me that I must learn to kick with both feet. That it's a skill that will set me above the pack. He's spent a lot of time with me just taking shots. I scored the winning goal in our game last night — with my left foot! Magic, Mom — it works!"

I began to notice how they were spending more time together, how James would often head down the basement stairs with his chess set under his arm. When I asked, he said, "I was having a game with Fred."

On Sundays I usually made an effort to cook an evening meal and we ate together then as a family. I tried to make it a special time, a properly cooked meal around a properly laid table and with proper table manners. Sometimes, James invited Fred to eat with us and that was usually pleasant.

That was how it was for their teenage years. I trusted them to do what was right in my absence — until one day I came home early with a bad headache and heard grunting and groaning coming from upstairs. I recognized immediately what was happening. I dropped my briefcase in the hall, ran up the stairs two at a time and threw open the bedroom door. There was so much activity that they didn't notice me right away. I just stood there in the doorway dumbfounded at the sight of a set of naked buttocks staring me in the face. At first I thought it was a stranger until I recognized the back of James's head, his face, well, never mind.... Lying prostrate on the bed was a female form, a set of large pale breasts splayed in both directions. The air was ripe with heat and odour. That is my memory of the scene. Then the female on the bed opened her eyes and saw me.

"Up, darling." She clipped James around the ear and treated me to a slow sardonic smile.

James sat back, his hand reaching for his groin.

"Not that, silly boy." She shoved James aside and propped herself up on both elbows. "Christ, woman, don't you ever knock?" She tapped my otherwise preoccupied son on the shoulder and pointed in my direction as if the mailman had arrived with a delivery.

"Out!" I moved further into the room avoiding the various items of clothing on the floor and ignoring James as if he simply was not there. The woman uncoiled herself, modesty not a priority, and sitting on the side of the bed reached with a long shapely leg for the purple dress on the floor, picked it up expertly with her toes and allowed the slippery stuff to fall easily over her head and shoulders to her waist. She then stood up and with a slight tug or two it fell down over her naked body. Zzzzip, and the operation was complete. When she stooped to pick up her other bits and pieces of clothing I had a fierce urge to kick her ample rump and put a swift end to her staged performance. Instead, I picked up her scuffed red stilettos and flung them out onto the landing. At the door she turned, puckered up and blew a mock kiss to a very startled James.

"Energetic boy!" She winked at me before sailing off down the stairs.

I began a tirade, "How dare you —" but he quickly shut me down.

"If I am to continue living here, I need some freedom, so get used to it, Mom. Just because in your day young people never had sex before marriage doesn't mean that we have to stay virginal."

Before things became any more complicated I left the room.

The following evening, I saw him walk home from soccer in close conversation with Fred. Later he came to me and said, "I'm sorry, Mom, I'll be more discreet in future."

James was seventeen at the time and preparing to write his final exams at school. He still had his sights set on being an accountant and had applied to university. He decided to stay in St. John's, supposedly, "to watch out for me," but there were no other choices — the money was not there to go elsewhere and he didn't get any scholarships. I was beginning to map out a role for him in the business.

"Claire spends too much time alone, Mom. It's not good. She doesn't talk to me anymore unless she wants something."

This is what James told me one Sunday evening as we cleared up after dinner. Claire had left the table abruptly as soon as we had finished eating and had gone upstairs to her room.

"She needs help. When I tried to talk to her yesterday, she actually pushed me out of her room and locked the door."

I was aware of the growing problem but had done nothing about it. I suggested removing the lock. "That's not a solution," he said. "Call Dad's friend, Dr. White, he's a psychiatrist. He may help."

"I can't possibly do that. The whole town — "

"Stop, Mom, stop right there." He actually raised his hand. "Call him."

He got up then and began to flip through the telephone book. He was trembling as he wrote down the number. "Do it, Mom. Do it now or I will."

It was me who took the brunt of her anger. At first she wanted nothing to do with Dr. White. However, with his help and kindly manner and the fact that he had been her father's friend, he managed to get her to cooperate. I was glad I made the move that night, but I attribute

Claire's current well-being and stability to James. Her possible slide into depression was stalled and she did manage to come through her final years at school in a much improved state of mind. She got some sizable scholarships but not the really big ones we had hoped for and went away to McGill University in Montreal. It was a surprising move — but then, Claire never followed the crowd. She had decided on a career path — science and then medicine.

I'm not sure how, but by some miracle, my youngest child had found her way.

I have agreed to work with the physiotherapist and I am making progress. I can now go up and down the corridor unescorted. Fortunately, I still have some vision and if I go carefully, I can just about manage on my own. At the end of the corridor, I usually pause briefly in the doorway to the common room so I can deliberately turn my back on the row of inert residents who sit in a semi-circle around the walls staring at the television. I want to establish clearly that I am not one of them.

One day last week, when I was walking the corridor, I heard music, piano music, coming from the same room so I ventured far enough into the room to see what was going on. The residents had all gone to lunch but someone to my right was playing softly on a piano.

"It has a lovely tone," a man's voice said. "Do you play?"

"Yes,"' I said, "but only for myself."

He went on to tell me that lunch time and mid-afternoon was a good, quiet time to come and play.

I turned to leave.

"Come again. I like to play for someone. I'm here Monday, Wednesday and Friday."

I asked Eleanor about him.

"He finds playing to be therapeutic," she said. "If you want to try I'll take you there this afternoon when most people are napping or early evening before I go home — most people have retired for the night by then."

It was her way of coaxing me towards some measure of independence. She insists I can still do what I have always done. "You'll just do it differently. It takes a little help from others and willingness on your part." Then she added, "Dad still plays the accordion even though he has low vision." I wish I could believe her.

After dinner that evening, when everyone had retired, I did go and fumble around on the piano for fifteen minutes or so, trying to find a tune. I loved the feel of the keys beneath my fingers and I thought if only I could quickly find middle C and G and F sharp my fingers might find their own way. I wanted to play. Eleanor kept assuring me I could. I promised to think about it, but that was more to please her than with any real expectation of results.

Claire's move to Montreal proved to be a good one for her. She was doing extremely well academically and was happy. She had also made a startling discovery.

She had been there three years and was about to graduate with a science degree and invited me to attend her graduation. This was somewhat of a surprise, for she had never discussed her program, her marks, or any aspect of her college life with me. At Christmas when she came to visit for a few days, she was relaxed and seemingly content. But one could never be sure with Claire. She was still quiet but not so withdrawn, and we had some pleasant conversations. At the time I had more money to spend and tried to interest her in a few of the trendy chain stores that had opened in the city since she had left, but she wasn't interested. I bought her an outfit for Christmas that I thought would suit her figure and colouring but she never wore it. She had taken an interest in cooking and I shared a few tips and recipes with her. That was about it. Connecting with her was like struggling with two short ends of string and trying every which way to tie a knot.

"I like to read and study," she told me when I tried to inquire about her life.

"I have some good friends and we talk and listen to music. That's all I need." I had been cautioned not to put pressure on her but to be supportive and positive, so that was what I tried to do. I didn't feel welcome, so I was reluctant to invade her world. I wasn't wholehearted about attending the graduation but James insisted I do so.

"Go. Show her you're proud of her accomplishments. Haven't you noticed, your daughter is brilliant, Mom."

"She works hard, James." This was not meant as a criticism but I could see it was perceived as one.

"You, of all people, should understand. Where were your parents when you needed them? She wants your approval. Don't you get it?"

James could be so cruel when angry. This time the thrust went deep and instantly invoked a chilling memory — a cozy drawing room, the deep-blue vase filled with yellow daffodils, the chiselled perfection of my mother, my father's callous words lying about the room like loose change, the anomaly that was life at Kilgraney — a life of privilege that scorned the very meaning of the word.

With some misgivings, I travelled to Montreal for Claire's graduation and an extraordinary encounter.

Her friends were an unusual group, very laid back and unconventional but obviously fond of Claire and very proud of her achievements. One young man in the group seemed to single me out for attention. He was charming, taking pains to see that I had a drink, introduced me all around and included me in conversations. When I first met him I couldn't take my eyes off the matted ropes of black hair; held together with a rubber band at the nape of his neck, they hung all the way down his back to his waist. Later I learned that these are called dreadlocks. He was otherwise a striking young man, clean shaven with a pleasant face and dark intelligent eyes. He had been introduced to me as Harley. "My friends call me Har." His smile was gentle and sincere. He was a musician.

I was invited to dine with the group that evening at a small restaurant on Rue St. Denis. Claire and I walked there, stopping along the way to purchase a few good wines to share with her friends. It was a French restaurant and I was surprised when she told me that, at this restaurant, you could bring your own wine. I sat beside Har and he helped me choose from the menu, telling me his favourites. I chose pan-fried tilapia. It was a fish I was not familiar with and he assured me it was delicious. In the course of the evening, when Claire was otherwise distracted, I plucked up the courage to ask, "How do you wash your hair?"

He laughed. "That's what everyone wants to know. Simple," he said. "Just wash it. It's all dead anyway. It's the scalp that needs attention." He flicked his tail of hair as if batting a fly. We chatted some more and after a few glasses of wine I dared to ask why he chose this hairstyle.

"I think it suits me." He laughed, showing a very fine set of teeth. "You can feel it." He turned his head around.

I could see how matted it was and when I touched it, it was like boiled wool. "And what does your mother think?"

He turned to face me. "It doesn't bother her."

He was charming and very easy company and I managed to have a very pleasant evening.

The following morning, as Claire prepared omelets for breakfast, I wanted to tell her I was proud of her and that I wished her father had been there to witness her success but I couldn't get the words out properly. They came in spurts and starts as if being squeezed out of me like toothpaste from a tube — too much, too little. Dreadful! Then I said something I hadn't intended saying and made things worse. "Your achievement may spur James on to do better."

"Do stop comparing us, Mummy. James is doing very well." She smacked another smooth, brown egg on the side of a bowl and began to beat furiously with a wire whisk.

"I noticed you and Har having quite the chat."

"I like him," I said. "He's charming, except of course for the hair." That popped out again without thought; grist for another dust up.

She was chopping mushrooms and green onions, brandishing a chef's knife with a degree of competence that was both admirable and alarming.

"Did he tell you about his connection to Newfoundland?" She said over the din.

"No."

The chopping continued and then she calmly put down the knife and turned to me.

"I'm glad that you like Har, Mummy."

"He's not your boyfriend, is he?"

She laughed casually, wiping her hands on a checkered cloth. Back then she wore multiple rings, on her chubby fingers.

"I'm not sure if you want to know this, Mummy. She was fiddling with the rings again, arranging them as if they were a special exhibit.

"Har's father has Daddy's lungs."

She spoke with such cool assurance I thought for a moment she was playing with me, getting back at me for past comments. But her gaze was steady and her eyes very bright. Then I thought, someone is taking advantage of her, she has been seduced into believing that ... any number of weird possibilities scrambled my thoughts.

"How can you possibly know that? No one knows that."

She sat down across the table from me and focused again on the rings.

"Claire, look at me."

"It's true, Mummy. He is alive and lives here in Montreal. I have met him."

"Claire, you should know better than to pay attention to such nonsense."

But her head tipped to one side and she was trying to make me look at her and I didn't want to look at her.

"Mummy." Her hand was on mine and when I eventually looked up, her gaze was very earnest. "Remember the day we went to the hospital to say good-bye to Daddy? Well, that night when you and James had gone to bed, I went back downstairs. I wanted to be alone. The day's newspaper was lying unopened on the table. I picked it up and began to turn the pages, not looking for anything in particular. A fairly large picture on page three caught my eye. It was a photograph of a container about the size of one of those hard coolers. It was tied around by a bungy-cord and was lying on the tarmac at the airport. Underneath were the words, *Precious Cargo on its way to Toronto*."

All the while Claire was stroking my hand.

"That container was carrying transplant organs going from St. John's to Toronto. Unknown to the workers, it had fallen off a trolley."

I tried to pull away but she tightened her grip, watching carefully, judging my reaction.

"I didn't imagine it. Honestly," she said, "but it had to contain Dad's organs."

She paused to give me time to absorb this information and then continued.

"I stood there in the kitchen feeling like I had been transported to some unearthly place I didn't know. I kissed the picture and felt so guilty, like I was wrong to have come back down the stairs. I wasn't supposed to see all this. I ripped up the paper then and stuffed it deep into the garbage bin and went back upstairs."

She told me she had cried all night thinking about him. "I couldn't tell anyone," she said, "not even James. I knew what everyone would say, that it was all in my imagination."

"I need a cigarette, Claire," I said, knowing well how she forbade smoking in her apartment, but she got up and put a saucer on the table in front of me. As I inhaled she continued to tell me how one day, shortly after she arrived in Montreal, she had met Har. As they got to know each other they talked about their families. He told her that his dad had had a lung transplant and she told him about her Dad and then about what she had seen in the newspaper. "It was so good to share it with someone," she said. "You can just imagine where the conversation went from there. It was only a matter of exchanging dates and we knew."

How is it that suddenly, out of nowhere, the past pops up, bald-faced and uninvited? I am in the funeral home standing beside Jack's coffin. It is Jack in there, right down to the white handkerchief in his breast pocket but inside I know he is empty. Beneath the neatly pressed jacket, there is a big hollow cavern. Every organ is gone, every string of tissue scooped out, harvested, sent away and I wonder if I touch him will he feel different, if I press on his abdomen will it collapse under my hand? And I feel panic rise in me and I touch a safe place, his cheek, and it is cold and pale and firm. I want to lean over and kiss his face and whisper *you live in another, my darling, in several others.* And then the old tortured plea. Did I do the right thing?

I forced myself back to reality and stared at my daughter. She had a haunted look about her. How often had I imagined Jack's heart beating warm and strong in someone else's chest, nursed the idea of his lungs continuing to rise and fall, pink and healthy and full of clean, life giving oxygen. Time and time again, I assured myself that somewhere, a father was restored to his children, a young man returned to his wife, any number of scenarios came to me. What if a woman had been the recipient of his heart, his lungs?

"Would you like to meet him, Mummy?"

"Meet who?"

"Har's dad. He'd like to meet you. If you wish, of course."

I remember the sun on the glass bowl, the yellow eggs swirling about, scrambled like my thoughts. This man is real, alive, a part of Jack. He wants to meet me. Claire has met him. I have touched his son's hair. Suppose I don't like him?

I stubbed out my cigarette and excused myself.

I went for a walk, feverishly unravelling the conversation in my mind. Time was short. I was leaving the next day. Without realizing, I arrived outside the restaurant where we had eaten the previous day. I stood at the window looking past my reflection and remembering Har, his smile, the wooly head of hair, his pleasant gentle way. Had he felt obligated, beholden? I pushed the door open and took the nearest seat available and ordered an espresso.

I suppose curiosity got the better of me. I had the time, and maybe the opportunity would never arise again. I liked Har.

"I'll meet with him," I told Claire when I returned, "at the restaurant on St. Laurent where we had dinner, ten o'clock tomorrow morning. I have a flight to catch later on in the afternoon. We can have a coffee, and if necessary, I can make a quick but polite exit. I want no hoopla, no introductions. I'll handle this myself."

"Excellent! Just look for an older, more substantial version of Har — without the dreadlocks," she added, a mischievous smile circling her mouth.

"I'll be wearing a red jacket. Please let him know."

I walked the route again and got there slightly ahead of schedule. I glanced around the restaurant for a likely candidate, saw none and took a seat in a booth towards the back with a view of the door. I began to remove my coat, remembered it was my ID and settled in to wait. The restaurant was almost empty. A young man entered, followed soon after by a burly-looking fellow done up in leathers, a large helmet tucked under his arm. I decided to study the menu while I waited.

"Mrs. Drodge?" The voice was smooth and warm like melted chocolate.

I looked up. "Yes."

"Bill Palladini," he said, "Har's dad."

"A biker!" I may have breathed the word but I'm not sure if it ever left my lips. He appeared to hear because he tucked his helmet under his arm and drew back his shoulders into a slightly comic pose. For a minute I thought he might salute.

He gave a soft laugh, relaxed and thrust his hand out across the table. I placed my fingers on his palm. His grip was compelling. He peeled off the black leather jacket, straining a little with the effort, and threw it on the seat beside him. The helmet he anchored with more care within the folds of the jacket. He sat down, shifting about on the seat until he was quite comfortable. I followed his every move, more taken aback than interested. I tell you now that had an ostrich come through that door and taken a seat across from me I couldn't have been more surprised. Having shed the leather, he was slimmer than he appeared at first glance. He was a big man carrying a little extra weight around his middle. A reddish crease made by the helmet burned on his forehead.

"Coffee?" he asked, but he had already turned away calling out to the waitress as I nodded. He then leaned on the table looking at me with an amused grin. "Claire didn't tell you. Did she? I'm not your ordinary guy."

"No she did not." I was pleased that my tone reflected my annoyance. What he had to say next sounded like a carefully worded speech that needed to be spoken right away before the opportunity passed.

"I am here, alive and well, because of your generosity. When they offered me a new lung, I was shocked, just as shocked as you are now. A gang member with a reputation, a record and a beer-belly is not a likely

candidate or so I thought. I had no serious addictions, but I was a user."
He saw my reaction. "I'm sorry, Sylvia, Mrs. Eh —"

"Drodge," I said.

"Yes."

The coffee had arrived and he continued, looking more subdued by the minute yet determined to say his piece. "I know I didn't deserve it but it wasn't just handed to me." I could see that he was nervous, anxious to have his say before being cut off. "I had to get in shape, eat properly, exercise, get clean. There were pages of instructions, strict guidelines and if I didn't meet their criteria I could forget it. It just wasn't going to happen. Well," he said sitting back, "the short version is that I did what was asked of me and I got a lung. Your husband's lung."

"I see."

"I wanted to meet you, Mrs. Drodge," he said, "and say thanks. I never did think I'd have the chance to do this but I swear to God every night of my life, before I drop off, I put my hand here on my chest and bless the person who gave me another crack at life, a chance to sort things out."

It was my turn to feel uncomfortable. I had no wish to speak of Jack or my own experience of the transaction or whatever one might call it. I was beginning to regret my decision to meet with him.

"Being close to death is a real kick in the head," he continued. "It made me see what was important. I became a father to Har, a real father. I didn't deserve the opportunity but it happened." He went on to tell me that it was a wonderful thing for someone in my situation to have done, to be able to think of others and care so much.

What was I supposed to say to that? All I could do was feel awkward and begin to make my exit. But he was not finished.

"I'm not a bad sort, but I'm no angel either," he said. "At one time, my bike and 'the gang' was all I cared about. My wife, and Har, came second. She left me when I got sick. Took Har with her but later we hooked up again. He's a great young man. Talented too."

As soon as he stopped to draw a breath, I said, "Pardon me, but did you say gang?"

"Yes, I did, not the *Angels* or the like, no badges, no colours, just a gang." He said this in a dismissive way as if it made everything all right. This was beyond me; a gang member, sitting across the table from me, admitting to doing "some bad things" and tapping his chest and saying "but nothing since." Then horror of horrors!

"I've been inside — break and enter, mostly."

"Break and enter." This tid-bit slipped out, I believe, unintentionally. I almost missed it. I was still trying to sort out the gangs and the badges and colours.

What was happening was bizarre, like watching a short episode of *Strange but True* on television: you gape, you listen and then you gape some more. Then he began to smooth over the edges like one might smooth a cake mixture in a pan prior to popping it in the oven.

"I was just a kid at the time."

"Just a kid!" I said, "but old enough to own and ride a motor cycle."

"Well…" He smiled and shrugged his shoulders. The prepared speech, at this point, was over and now he was in an appeasing mode, justifying or maybe even apologizing for his past. I was at a loss.

"I got sense," he said. He made a fist with one hand and with the other began to squeeze his locked fingers as if limbering up for a fight. There was a loud crack and then another and each time I jumped.

"I got sense knocked into me. I went and got myself a trade."

I was afraid of this man. It was nothing I could put my finger on, but those locked fists with the tufts of black hair pointed to an undercurrent of unpredictability that I thought might surface at any moment. After all he had been "inside." In the old days, apart from being frightened, I doubt I would have even dreamed of engaging him in conversation. But I have to admit I was intrigued and wanted to know more about him. I was, after all, a professional woman now and used to dealing with working men who could be rough, so I decided to stand my ground.

All this time, he continued to eye me like a great black bear that had suddenly encountered an uncommon species.

I sat back in the booth pointedly, allowing my eyes to take in the fading, fiery ring on his forehead, the collar of straight black hair that flared above the neck of his T-shirt, the thick, black fuzz that spread like ground cover over his arms through the maze of purple tattoos and onto his fingers. I made no effort to conceal my interest in the way he constantly held his left hand, Napoleon style, flat to his chest, openly displaying his dirty fingernails. I was being rude, I knew, but I didn't care. When I had finished my inspection I raised my eyes.

"I'm a mechanic," he said, without flinching.

"I own a plumbing business." I don't know why I said this.

"I know. Claire told me. She thinks her mother's got guts."

"She does?"

He smiled in a companionable sort of way. He had thrown me a line and I caught it. He talked and I listened. He told me about his bike and what is was like to ride a powerful machine. He spoke passionately about the freedom, the independence, the roar of the wind when "doin' a hundred and fifty" on the highway, the smell and feel of the air, the sting of driving rain, how it blurs the vision, sometimes obscuring it altogether.

"It's part of the thrill." He laughed.

"Reckless!"

"Nothing like it. I can move faster than others on the road. The big fast cars, the police — I zip past, weave in and out and leave them behind. It drives them crazy. I see it in their faces as I accelerate and whiz by. They can't catch me. I'm gone! I don't have to wait in traffic. The satisfaction lies in playing with danger, the chase. It may sound crazy but —"

"No it doesn't." Gutsy me jumped in. "I know exactly what you mean. Until I came to Canada I rode horses. The hunt was thrilling, dangerous, but a hundred and seventy kilometers an hour on hard tarmac, on a motorcycle, that is just reckless!"

"No more than clearing a fence at full gallop, astride a jittery animal that stands another six feet off the ground. Some of them jumps in the shows you see on the television are six or seven feet high. The animal must weigh hundreds of pounds. Now, I've never set my backside on a horse but I know it would scare the shit outta me." He leaned into the table. "You do have guts. Claire is right."

The coffee had turned cold but I took a gulp to hide the pleasure I was feeling. I'm interesting and exciting and gutsy. Spunk! I took another gulp of cold coffee and began to tell him bits and pieces about my life back then, exciting bits mostly. I hinted at high-level competition, national championships, trophies, medals, challenges.

"Your crowd must be rich, animals like that cost a few bucks."

"And your bike?" I said.

"True. I came by a bit of money one day and I bought a 1978 Harley — my lifelong dream." A shadow crossed his face. "I paid the price for her," he said in a more serious tone. "She was worth it," he said perking up. "She's a beauty. That's how Harley got his name. I was always mad about bikes, especially the Harley. I could think of no better name for my boy."

"An expensive toy!" I was pressing the point, pushing for more information, knowing there was more to tell and unwilling to let go.

"Not a toy, not my machine!" He cracked his knuckles again.

I tensed.

"My bike is my partner. I care about her. When something is wrong, I can sense it, feel it. I talk to her and she urges me to listen. Taking care of my bike is like a religion, it's important to me. Sometimes, I just strip her down, examine each part, clean and polish it and then carefully put her all back together again. When I hear that contented purr, the pleasure is there. I know everything about her. She has her own life."

There and then I was back in the stables at Kilgraney, Saoirse, my partner, sweating, restless, tender, reassuring words whispered in her ear, a coarse brush combing her sweating flanks, the soft touch of her as she muzzled my neck, the contented rhythmic breathing as she settled down.

"I understand," I said

"About me and the bike?"

He didn't wait for an answer. "I had an accident once; a blow out on the 401 just outside of Kingston. It was my own fault; lack of maintenance, the tire was old: I was careless. It's never the fault of the bike."

I was beginning to feel the old thrill of danger, that wild sensation of flirting with eternity and then relief, the moment when you are clear and back in control, safe until the next time. I might have told him then about my horse, about the hunt, even breathed some of my own secrets, the near misses, the foolish risks, the moment when the terrier hauls the fox from his den, the excitement of the kill, the closeness of horse and rider — but time came to the rescue. I had completely lost track. I jumped up, our meeting at a sudden end. "I have a flight to catch," I said.

"I'd offer you a ride if I had an extra helmet."

At that moment, I knew that had a helmet, by some miracle, appeared out of the blue, I'd have rode pillion behind him for the sheer hell of it with no thought of where I was going or what I was doing. We shook hands and said goodbye and I fled to catch a taxi.

"Well," Claire said when I rushed in the door, "how was it?"

"Fine, but how could you possibly think I would want to meet such a person."

She laughed.

Just as it seemed that problems connected with the development of our oil industry were being worked out, another crisis occurred. The cod fishery, mainstay of the Newfoundland economy, collapsed and put rural Newfoundland in crisis. Around the bays and inlets, small communities were shutting down, workers were moving away or being retrained for jobs that did not exist. In the fledgling oil industry, centered mainly in St. John's, there were rumblings about the problems connected with the construction of the huge Hibernia oil rig. Experienced construction workers in the oil industry were being imported from outside the province. Costs were escalating. There were new concerns being expressed about the wisdom of anchoring a giant oil rig to the ocean floor in the iceberg filled waters two hundred miles off our coast. Construction of the platform and operating costs were expected to be in the billions. The development of the Hibernia oil field was being touted as the most expensive and perilous oil project ever undertaken.

The stability of Newfoundland as a place to do business was in question. It was all deeply unsettling.

It was the only topic at the Board of Trade luncheons. There was scant comfort to be had in the knowledge that just about everyone was hurting. We had just started phase two of our renovation. Vinyl siding had been ordered for the outdoor sheds and main building and there were renovations underway to the main entrance. The past twelve years had been the most productive and satisfying years of my whole life. The business plan, the ideas, the renovations were all coming together. We were just about there, and now this. I had saved the business and had continued to turn a profit, keeping the bank happy and me with an income. I had not yet begun to reap real financial benefits but I felt a great sense of accomplishment.

In moments of generosity, thoughts of my father sometimes crossed my mind. I reluctantly gave him credit for recognizing my potential as a business woman. Having gained access to my head he kept returning to goad my conscience, harking back to my stupidity and lack of foresight. In a now prosperous Ireland, Kilgraney, with its acres of rich pasture land, was worth millions.

Cash flow became a major problem. The bank still owned seventy-five percent of my house and our stock was not moving off the floor. I was alarmed, shaken that things could turn around so rapidly. Every night I came home laced with anxiety and raw fear. Eating was out of the question so I smoked. I slept fitfully, waking in the night drenched in cold sweat.

James was by now a qualified chartered accountant, his sights set on becoming a partner. He was finally motivated to excel. I had an accountant and a doctor in the family. The children were both on the way to successful careers. This was the bright spot. Or so I thought.

James had opinions of course on how I should proceed. "Get rid of some of the dead wood, like McCarthy. He's been hanging around in that faded shop coat for too long and that little flirt in cash, she's cute but an embarrassment. The plumbers might like it but not your high-end clients."

I was taken aback by the raw aggression in his attitude and told him so, but at the same time I admired his assertiveness and was glad to have him there to advise me. I had transferred the accounting work to James's firm so he would be up to date on our activities and give regular feedback on our progress. It also assisted him with building a client base. He had bought a small property close by in the downtown area so we spent many evenings going over the books and looking for places to cut costs. He took it upon himself to go through stacks of files and old boxes of records to better acquaint himself with the workings of the business. It was a relief to have a fresh young mind working alongside me again.

While I mulled over what action I should take, my thoughts went back to the idea of the 4Ms as put forward by my bank manager when I first set out in business: *markets, materials, money, management.* At that time, I was the weak link — now it was Mr. McCarthy. I was running the business. I understood the issues, the product, the markets and the clientele. It was up to me to find my way through this slowdown. The oil would still be in the ground, I reasoned, after the big boys had worked out their differences. In the meantime we, at James Drodge & Company, would have to pull together. Where necessary, the sales staff, in particular Mike, would have to pick up the slack.

James thought he might object. "Not part of the job description," he said.

"Then he too will have to go," I countered, wishing I felt as confident and in control as I sounded.

When I brought up the subject of compensation for Mr. McCarthy, James dismissed the idea.

"Find a reason to fire him. That will take care of the problem. A week's notice with pay. He won't put up a fight. Trust me. This is business. You must be tough." A smile that invited conspiracy touched the corner of his mouth. I was being herded towards a short-cut that was not to my liking and it bothered me.

"James," I said, "perhaps you don't realize it, but this is more than just a business to me. Right now, it is who I am. I have been told once too often that I may fail, that I am a woman and that a woman like me could not succeed. Well, I have succeeded and many think admirably. I am not about to let go. Don't try to undermine me, James."

It was a tense moment. The pressure and lack of sleep was making me edgy and overly cautious. I was vulnerable once more. This time I fully understood the dire consequences of failing.

Firing employees did not come easily to me. It made me realize how much I had changed. I had come to appreciate and respect hard work and loyalty. I had come to recognize that there were other considerations, things I could no longer ignore. I was aware that Mr. McCarthy's circumstances — his age, his disability — placed him in a difficult position when looking for employment. He had a family, a wife and eight children, some of whom were still of school age.

In the old days I would have brushed this aside. It was not my concern but I had experienced the terror of being close to destitute and could not ignore it in others. It distressed me to let this loyal, hardworking man go. I had witnessed and admired his willingness, under duress, to change and adapt to new ways. He had handled the situation in a gentlemanly and competent manner and had always treated me with the utmost respect. But when it came down to making the decision there was no doubt in my mind, the business had to come first.

He came into my office equipped as usual with his clipboard, the customary ribbon of coloured pencils neatly arranged in the breast pocket of his overalls. His withered hand, hanging loosely by his side, seemed more noticeable than usual. I had considered carefully what needed to be said so when he was seated, I went straight to the point. The look of utter shock and disbelief on his face is what I remember most.

"When?" he said on hearing what I had to say.

"One week's notice as of today, in addition to one month's pay." I spoke briskly, my conscience chiding me. "I am frightfully sorry. It is simply unavoidable. We have to cut costs." Then he said something that totally shocked me.

"What about the house?"

"The house? What are you talking about?"

He told me that the house he had lived in since he got married was given to him by Jack's father to mark twenty-five years of service to the company.

"It was in lieu of a pension," he said. "He bought it for me. I was to take full possession on retirement from the company."

"I know nothing about this," I said. "Do you have the deeds?"

"I tell you, full possession on retirement. That was the agreement. He kept the paper in safe keeping for when I retired. I saw that paper with my name on it. I have never paid a cent of rent for that house from that day on."

"Did my husband know about this?" I was beginning to feel I was caught up in a whirl of ambiguity.

"That I don't know. I didn't see too much of Dr. Drodge."

He had become agitated, his eyes roving around like a fly looking for a spot to land.

"I was sixteen when I got my start here," he said. "I came in here the very day I finished school, stood right in this office and asked for work. I wanted to be here ahead of the others. Everyone was looking for work. I knew him to be a decent man and thought he might give me a chance. He asked me what I could do. I thought that to be a good sign. At least he hadn't taken one look and shut the door on me. So I said, 'I'm quick with numbers. I can show you.'"

He was speaking louder than was his custom, rushing on telling me how Mr. Drodge had picked up a detailed invoice from his desk and asked him to check and see if the total was correct. Which he did and when he had finished checking, he found the total to be incorrect by $100.26. It seems he was right and Jack's father offered him a job on the spot and he had worked with the company ever since.

It was a heartfelt story. Not one that was altogether familiar to me, but I gave him my word that I would look into the situation. When he stood to go, I noticed that the flash of bravado that had driven him to relate his story had passed. Standing there in his navy shop coat, clipboard hanging by his side, he looked reduced.

At the door he turned, "I saw that paper. My name was on it in black and white." He walked out the door, not bothering to close it behind him.

I got up and closed the door and went straight to look in the employee files. His name was Robert Joseph McCarthy. Born April 13, 1943. He was now fifty years old and had worked for James Drodge & Company for thirty-four years. His address was listed as 5 Cuddihy Street. I had no idea where the house was but I had a map in the car. I was about to slip out and get it but thought better of that idea and decided to wait until I got home. I went through the file on Joseph McCarthy carefully, but there was no sign of the piece of paper he had spoken of. I removed the file for Alice Neary.

Alice bounced into the office in her usual high spirits, took a seat without being asked and waited. She was clever and comical. I liked her in many ways but she tended to be too forward on occasions. It was she, I believe, who came up with the title of Lady Ballcock and knowing I had accepted the title, she had no qualms about using it. From time to time she would bob a playful curtsy as she presented me with tea first thing in the morning and say, "Tea, m'lady." She kept things lively around the office. She was one of the first to take a computer course at night and had volunteered to do secretarial work for me in order to practice her skills. She accepted her lay-off notice as if it was of little consequence but was adamant that she was entitled to a week's notice with two weeks' pay. "I have to find another job now. Don't I? " Rather cheeky, I thought. I found out later that she was about to leave anyway and had a job already lined up with the government.

So I was glad that I had stuck to my guns and given her a week with pay. I doubt she had any intention of giving me any notice. James was right that she was cunning.

That evening, I located the house in question on the map and immediately got in the car and drove by there. It was one of four attached, two-storey clapboard houses, located on one of those hilly side streets close to the harbour in the poorer section of St. John's. It was painted grey with a white trim and looked very basic but clean and orderly.

While I sat in my car across the street a young girl and an older woman came down the street and stopped outside No. 5. They were carrying bags of groceries. The woman set her bags down on the bottom step while the young girl went ahead to open the door. She came back, took the woman's arm and helped her up the three stone steps and in through the door. She then returned for the remaining groceries. I recall feeling slightly uncomfortable seeing mother and daughter in such close communion with each other. When the door closed behind them I drove away slowly, imagining the scene behind the closed door.

Several evenings, spent turning out drawers and cabinets and boxes looking for the paper that Mr. McCarthy spoke about, produced nothing. I phoned the Registry of Deeds. A rude woman, afraid I might make further demands on her time, told me that property doesn't have to be registered in Newfoundland. "And we don't search for deeds here either. A bill of sale is all you needs."

I remembered that James had spent some time going through boxes that had been cleared out of the office and wondered if he had seen it.

I called him at the office to tell him about the situation and ask if he was aware of any such paper. The silence at the other end prompted me to ask if he was still there.

"Yes, Mother, I'm still here. I'm thinking." His voice sounded flat and noncommittal. "That story sounds a bit farfetched to me. If that ever took place the deeds would have been carefully filed away and registered. Besides, retirement age is sixty-five. The man cannot be anywhere near that age."

"He's fifty, but he is being laid off now."

"Let him find another job. I suggest you leave it alone and let things settle down. The house is of no great value. Let him stay on there for now. Prices are rising. I'm sure that something will come to light sooner or later."

I began to explain that, at fifty years of age and with a disability, jobs were not easily come by, but he cut me off, saying, "Must run!" And then he was gone. I wondered afterwards how he knew the house was of no great value.

I did continue my search and found the name of a lawyer, a Mr. Anthony Dawson, on some papers. I called the number I was told that he had retired. I called his home. Yes, he had handled Mr. Drodge's affairs but knew nothing about the house in question. I had my doubts as to whether he remembered Mr. James Drodge.

When I explained the result of the search to Mr. McCarthy, he reiterated that he had seen the paper with his name. This time he was more forceful. I told him I would continue the search regarding the house but until the situation was cleared, things would continue as usual.

On the day he retired, we had a celebration in my office and I presented him with his cheque and spoke highly of his years of loyal service. It was a sad little affair. Alice Neary didn't bother with good-byes — she had taken up her new position with government that morning. I watched from my office window as the staff left for the day. There was no sign of him. Shortly afterwards he appeared in the yard carrying a small box tied with a string under his good arm. He walked down the laneway, turned right at the gate, and headed down the street for the last time and I wondered what goes through a man's mind on such an occasion.

Afterwards I wished I hadn't been so hasty in letting Mr. McCarthy go. Shortly thereafter it was announced that the federal government had acquired a twenty-five percent share in the Hibernia project. Once more we were on the move, disaster averted.

James married later that year. I was pleased with his choice. Having toyed for several years with what I considered to be unsuitable women, I was delighted when he chose Marianne Duhamel, a very attractive French-Canadian girl from a very well-to-do family. They were involved with land acquisition and real-estate holdings. The two met while at school in Quebec and had met again when James went to Montreal on business. She came from an old Quebec family — when I say old, I mean their roots go back a couple of hundred years or so. James told me they refer to themselves as *pure laine*, identifying in some way or other with the original settlers, fur trappers or the like. "Well," I said, "I hope you told them about your family. The Bolfes go back hundreds of years. Your grandmother was —"

"I know, Mother, 'presented as a debutante at the court of his majesty, King something or other.' Nobody cares anymore, Mother. I'm a Drodge, remember?"

"I care, James, I care very much about my lineage and so should you. I must point out that, for some reason, your future bride considers her background, such as it is, to be important. You have told her?"

"Told her what?"

"About your background."

"Yes, Mother. It was a big selling point."

The sarcasm was evident, but I believe there was more truth than he cared to admit.

When I met the Duhamel family, I was agreeably surprised. They were, I noticed, more European than North American in their manners and ways. Their home was charming: French country in style with touches of true elegance here and there, like the carpets and the antique rosewood chiffonier I noticed in the dining room. I was welcomed and treated with deference and respect. My ability to speak French was a distinct advantage and remarked on particularly in social settings. I was able to explain how I had spent a year at finishing school in Paris.

Marianne was a Catholic and this presented a problem. *The Romans* — this is a rather vulgar term, but nonetheless appropriate — can be such a trying lot, so resolute and infernally pig-headed in their ways. Much to my horror, James agreed to become a Catholic and to raise my grandchildren as Catholics. To say the least, having to digest this pill left me deeply troubled and exasperated. I had to address the subject with her father.

"I suppose I shall be permitted to enter *La Basilique De Notre Dame*, to attend my son's wedding?" I said. I knew a little of their service, being high-church myself, but I had heard rumours of unbelievers being compelled to wait outside the church during services. Monsieur Duhamel was very solicitous of my concerns and utterly charming. He was a perfect gentleman.

"Madam Drodge," he bowed slightly, "not only permitted but escorted with full honours down the aisle. If I were not otherwise engaged, I should insist on doing the honours myself but my eldest son would be honoured to do so."

Although I spoke to him in French, he replied in excellent English and continued in English — unusual, in my experience, for a French man. He had such a charming accent and so handsome. It was difficult to be cross.

It was a truly beautiful wedding with every detail handled to perfection. Elegance was the order of the day, and Marianne set the tone throughout with poise and grace. Her mother wore deep rose, a well-cut dress, which complemented her slightly plump figure. I wore pale aqua silk, an exquisite designer dress with matching picture hat that I bought in New York for the occasion. I had made the trip especially although I could ill afford such luxury. But I had to do this for my son.

James, more than ever, looked like his father — not the most handsome groom, but seeing him that morning at the altar, standing tall and erect, impeccably dressed in a well-cut morning suit, I realized he had my bearing. Throughout the service I endured, without a murmur, all the Popery, but when the priest raised his two fingers to bless my James, I looked the other way.

Claire, the only other family member present on the big day, arrived looking as Claire always did, underdressed and dowdy although she had made an effort with her hair. I glanced around the church, noting the obvious presence of money and style. I felt confident but wished Claire had consulted me about her dress. By her side and complete with dreadlocks neatly tied behind with a black satin ribbon to blend with his rented formal wear was Har Palladini, whom she had introduced to the company the previous evening as her partner. He looked quite distinguished and attractive in his own way. Being a musician one can get away with being a tad eccentric. I was taken aback of course by the news that they were now partners, which then, like now, can mean just about anything. Earlier, I had taken the trouble to identify a young architect, a cousin of the bride, whom I thought might make a possible match for Claire but when I suggested to James that he introduce him to his sister, he just laughed and said, "Certainly, Mother." I knew he had no intention of doing so.

"Do you intend to marry Har?" I asked Claire when the opportunity arose.

"And go along with all this foolish nonsense! Not on your life. Fine for James but I couldn't abide having all this rubbish foisted on me." At the time, she was on full scholarship at McGill, doing graduate work. What her mother thought or wanted was of no consequence, but the bitterness in her attitude did pain me.

Still, on that splendid day I had high hopes for my son.

Marianne moved to St John's and the couple settled into James's little clapboard house on Boggan Street. Of course it was not exactly Marianne's style, but she showed great flare in renovating and decorating the house and also remarkable foresight in predicting the rise in real-estate values in the city.

"It is in the me'dle of the city," she said in her charming French accent. "Location, location. We can make it very pretty and then sell it and buy a big house for James and me. Then we can have a bébé. Non?"

She hired a top-notch contractor to knock out walls, expose old brick, and put in a new kitchen and bathroom. The latter she ordered from James Drodge &Company. The interior design, right down to the colours and furnishings, was all her work. She then set about improving the outside and ordered bright yellow clapboard with cream trim and a berry-red door to be installed. It looked very attractive. Despite the slowdown in the economy, the little house sold as soon as it hit the market. They made a handsome profit and bought a lovely old house on Waterford Bridge Road at a very good price, where she proceeded to do the same thing.

I had expected to be reimbursed for the cost of the bathroom fixtures from the profits, but instead I was asked again to provide the materials for the next renovation. She wanted the best of everything, all of which had to be specially ordered. This time there were two bathrooms to be fitted, plus a powder room. When I balked at this she was surprised. "But, Bellemere" — this was how she had chosen to address me — "we have made a deposit with the profit and now we must make our home beautiful and important. Non?"

This time I made it quite clear. The materials could be purchased at cost but I expected cash on delivery. Marianne was furious and proceeded to pout and give Bellemere a tongue lashing in French, forgetting, or maybe not, that I understood French very well. When I mentioned the situation to James, I reminded him that we had laid people off to save money. He assured me that it was not a problem, that things would be taken care of, and I asked no more questions. As long as the bills were paid I didn't care where the money came from. Papa had deep pockets.

When she was done, the new home was simply stunning. Furniture and fabrics had been brought in from Montreal. Frequent buying trips back and forth were the order of the day, coupled with the occasional side trip, skiing in Colorado or The Laurentians where her parents had a chalet. In the spring it was the beach, always somewhere new and more exotic. I could hardly keep up with the excitement. They entertained in grand style and to my great delight, I was sometimes included. They were such a popular couple in the city, always on the go. It was exactly what I had longed for so much in my day.

Soon it was not enough for Marianne. She wanted James to seek a transfer to the Montreal office. I couldn't understand her discontent. It seemed to me that she had everything. A transfer was arranged, though not to Montreal but to Toronto, where a position was available. The beautiful house was sold, a handsome profit made. Marianne was content to be closer to Papa and Maman but James seemed unsure about the move. Once more I was on my own.

I got to thinking that maybe I should do the same with my house: new bathrooms might be a good idea. It was a luxury I could not afford just then, but I persuaded myself that I really did need to do some updates and this was a good place to start, especially with the current supply of stock on hand that had not moved for a while. I made up my mind that when things picked up again and the renovations on the business were complete, my house was to be my priority. It was in a prime location downtown, overlooking the harbour and city. It could be a very attractive residence.

With the reduction in staff, I was working long hours to keep up with the extra demands. There was no time for social activity. My only pleasure was playing the piano in the evenings for thirty or forty minutes before heading to bed to do some more work. Max was my constant companion. He was by then fifteen years old and very arthritic and I knew in my heart his time was up. I made the decision to have him put to sleep. The night before, I brought his cushion into the living room and placed it by the piano and I played softly to him until bedtime.

Alone again in my empty house, I missed Fred's modest presence. His calm assurance, his uncanny knack for knowing exactly what to say or do in a given situation had been so comforting. When he wrote that I had been an inspiration to him, I began to think of him differently, maybe even as a friend. But it was too late. He was gone. And who could blame him? Wherever he was, I wanted him to be safe — that is to say, I hoped he was warm and dry. That he had a place to live.

I need not have worried. While I worked at making a living in the plumbing business, Fred was carving out a significant career for himself. One afternoon, James was browsing in a small but prestigious gallery in Toronto. The gallery owner drew James's attention to a piece because the artist, Fredrick. J. McCoy, was from Newfoundland — though the owner was quick to add that the artist now lived and worked in Winnipeg but a few months previously had had a very successful showing at the gallery. The gallery owner was effusive, thrilled with the reviews. When James was handed some information on the artist, to his astonishment, the face that stared back at him was Fred's.

The gallery had two other pieces, which were brought out for James. It wasn't just the fact that Fred was the artist that shocked James, but also the nature of the work. "It was bold and bizarre, bordering on the surreal," he later told me. Even the signature penciled on the work, *Fredrick J. McCoy*, seemed strange.

James told the gallery owner that he had known Fred since he was a boy, that Fred had been his father's best friend — and that he could not imagine where inside the man this work had come from.

When I visited Toronto, James showed me the piece he had purchased. It was standing on the floor in his study.

"I can't say that I like it very much," he said as he propped it on a chair, "but I was told that two pieces from the collection had been purchased at the opening by a very reputable collector."

It was Fred's work, no mistake. I was mesmerized. In it the subject is a young native woman. The figure steps boldly out of darkness. The strange hawk-like features and the concentration of light on the face and feet is familiar. She is lean and angular. Sharp tines protrude from her scalp. On her right shoulder the gleaming barrel of a rifle catches the light. Power and defiance emanates from the woman. In marked contrast to these hard edges she wears a soft, cream-coloured robe fastened on the left shoulder by a smooth brown horn-shaped toggle. It falls in jagged edges to just below her knees. She moves forward with purpose. The title is *New Warrior*.

I recall James saying something about buying it as an investment.

I was bothered he had not seen fit to mention earlier that he had come across Fred's work.

"I didn't think you'd be interested," he said. "You never did like him."

Later I asked James to search the Internet to find out more. I wanted to understand what it was that he wished to say in his work. I learned he had taken to heart the plight of street people. Most of the pictures were very different from the one James had bought, and most were troubling, though not all. There were close-up images of people in dire distress, detailed and very evocative drawings of faces and bodies ravaged by loss and hardship but there were also faces full of strength and laughter and wisdom. Sometimes there was the suggestion in the work of intense memory of earlier times. Objects depicted from a past life were sometimes seen as if in a mirror or hidden in the work or even isolated from their real use or purpose. Frequently, as in *New Warrior*, images were distorted, not always in an obvious way but enough to demand that the person viewing the work pay close attention.

This new image of Fred as artist stayed with me and prompted me to search the *Globe and Mail* on a regular basis for any signs of other exhibitions or references to Fred and his work. When I travelled, I always checked local papers for news of him.

That afternoon in Toronto, as I contemplated Fred's remarkable rise in the art world, James surprised me by suggesting I sell the business and consider retiring. "What?" I said. "Sell everything I've worked for, now that the oil is finally close to production?"

He thought it was the perfect time to get out. "Take some time for yourself, Mom. The renovations are completed; the economic forecast is excellent, the business is turning a reasonable profit so it is a good time to sell."

At the time I was feeling exhausted. My life was one sided, all about work. I was approaching sixty and it was time I started living while I was still young and healthy enough to enjoy it. If I wished to continue in the business I had to consider other changes, particularly in the field of technology. We were lagging behind in this area and we needed to upgrade. It was something to think about.

James and Marianne were comfortably settled and I hoped this time it was permanent. Marianne was working in real estate, something to do with the family business. James was a junior partner with the firm. The Duhamel connection had obviously done wonders for his career, for he appeared to have very quickly acquired all the trappings of success. There was no bébé. I did not ask why.

Claire, too, seemed content doing her research. She showed remarkable promise although she rarely spoke of her work. She and Har now lived together in a two-bedroom rented apartment close to McGill University and the downtown. Their accommodation was sparse, their lifestyle simple. Claire's space was staked out by bookshelves and an ever increasing collection of technological devices. Har's space was defined by a guitar on a stand, a guitar case on the floor, several other instruments propped against a wall and a large keyboard.

When in Montreal, I enjoyed going to their place to share a meal in the tiny kitchen. There was always good food, wine, music and a constant run of conversation. Odd, lumpy chairs, thread-bare carpets, posters pinned to the walls gave the place a distinct feeling of impermanence. Nothing of importance, that I could see, was held in common.

It was during one of these visits, when I was alone with Claire, that she asked if I would like to meet Bill Palladini again.

"He asks about you," she said.

I immediately declined.

Later on, when I dared to think back on that meeting with Bill Palladini, I marvelled at the fact that at no time did I feel an emotional connection to Jack. That day in the cafe, the man who sat across the table from me, chatting and drinking coffee, did so with the help of Jack's lungs. Yet it meant nothing to me. They say that when a home is emptied of its inhabitants and their possessions, it loses its significance. Personal attachment fades and it becomes just another house, a shell. I wonder if this is a similar kind of detachment.

I can admit now that while I was fascinated, even excited, by Bill Palladini's personality and dangerous lifestyle, inwardly I squirm when I think about how I had openly allowed my eyes to travel over his muscular frame, blatantly staring at his massive tattooed arms and dirty fingernails, yet in my heart I knew I wanted to hop on the back of that Harley Davidson and ride away with him, down the Blvd. St. Laurent, weaving in and out of traffic, laughing, my red jacket flapping madly in the wind.

It did not come as a great surprise to me when a short time later Claire called to tell me she was off to Africa to work with Doctors Without Borders. With her education I thought it to be foolish and I told her so.

"People in Africa need well-educated doctors too," she scolded. "I can teach, share my skills and help to alleviate suffering. Isn't that what doctors are supposed to do?"

I told her that she needed to settle; to put down some roots. She told me it was too late for motherly advice. She tried to change the subject but I persisted, ignoring the rebuke.

"What about Har?" I asked.

She thought this was hilarious. "Har? Don't tell me you want me to marry him or some such foolishness," but added that she had asked him to come along. He had declined. When she reminded him that Africa had done wonders for Paul Simon's music career, he sensibly said, "Paul Simon had a career before he went there."

"He may come and visit me,"Claire said. End of conversation.

One month later she left for Somalia. I expect that Har is still in Montreal.

That evening I told James that I would consider his suggestion about retirement.

The physiotherapist says I'm doing really well. I can walk several lengths of the corridor and handle the stairs. I feel a lot more confident. I'm beginning to think Eleanor is right, that I need to stir myself, get up and get going while I still have some vision. She tells me constantly that, with some help, I will be able to function in my own house, use the stairs, bathe, dress, even cook and play the piano. I don't believe her. It all frightens me. I cannot understand how this can possibly be true without my eyesight. I get impatient and change the subject, but she continues to reassure me it is possible.

Granny's voice is still around. She whispers that I'm stubborn, willful, proud; a true Bolfe. It has taken me all these years to shake off her influence but she won't let go. Many times these qualities have stood me in good stead but now I fear they make my life impossibly difficult. Eleanor confirms this. She has this way of planting an idea in my head and then leaving it there to germinate.

As I contemplated plans for retirement, the house at 5 Cuddihy Street was on my mind. James had phoned suggesting that I take possession immediately and settle the question once and for all.

"What am I to do," I said, "put the man and his family out on the street?" James didn't reply but I knew that was what he had in mind.

Property values were a hot topic of conversation around town at the time. It was as if a virus had hit the city and everyone was infected. Every weed-ridden swamp and stony scrap of land now had value; fences that had long been trampled into the ground were suddenly upright again and new ones were popping up overnight. A hotel under construction in the city was to be taken down because it encroached by several inches on the adjacent property.

There was some justification for James's point of view. There was, after all, no proof of McCarthy's claim and I knew that James was increasingly concerned for me and my welfare. Change was happening at an alarming rate and it made me acutely aware of my age and vulnerability and the uncertainty of the business environment. My focus had been on the immediate future, the business, its success, its profitability, to the point that I had neglected my own needs. No longer sure as to the value of a small plumbing business in these uncertain markets, I was beginning to question the wisdom of having poured most of the profits back into it.

I gave the situation regarding the house on Cuddihy Street more thought than I care to admit. I struggled with the facts, the value of the property, the plight of the family, my own needs. I had come to value qualities like loyalty, hard work and dedication, and Mr. McCarthy exemplified these qualities. I could not bring myself to believe he was not speaking the truth. I hired someone, without telling James, to quietly investigate the history of the house — to talk to the neighbours, some old-timers who might remember something. Find out the story. There was not much information to be had but the opinion generally was that it was the McCarthy house, that they had lived there for years. No question about it.

I also spoke with Angela Fowler at her law office and asked her what she thought. She told me that, in her opinion, a judge would most likely look favourably on the claimant. The circumstances were unusual by present-day standards but back then it was not unheard of for a good employer to reward handsomely a valuable employee. In all likelihood, neighbours and friends would be called on to give evidence. "It could garner a lot of bad press," she warned. "It will not look good and you will probably lose."

Things came to a head sooner than I expected. I was informed via a letter from a legal establishment that in the continued absence of a deed of conveyance, that *Robert Joseph McCarthy having had: Open possession.... Exclusive use..... Notorious knowledge in the environs for over a period of more than twenty years, had applied for adverse possession (commonly known as squatters rights) of the property at 5 Cuddihy Street...,* etc. etc.

I was greatly taken aback by this aggressive approach. My first instinct was to phone and say so, but then I thought better of this idea and set aside the letter until I had time to collect my thoughts.

Around ten o'clock that evening I was at the piano, winding down the night when there was a knock on the front door. In the street light I recognized the familiar stance before I recognized the face beneath the dark ball cap. It was Mr. McCarthy.

"I was passing by," he said. "I heard the music — otherwise I would not have disturbed you at this late hour."

I ushered him into the living room where the light was on. I was glad to see him. Dealing with the situation face to face was much more to my liking than over the telephone. He removed his cap but refused to let me have his jacket or to take a seat.

"I had a letter today from your lawyer," I said.

He shifted.

"That was not my idea, Mrs. Drodge."

"But you engaged the lawyer."

"The lawyer in question is my daughter. She has just been called to the bar. She insisted when she saw the *For Sale* sign on the house."

"For Sale?"

"Yes, the For Sale sign."

I was shocked beyond belief and I was angry. Without thinking I said, "I know nothing of this. The house is *not* for sale. It will not happen. You can take my word for that."

He thanked me and left. I went straight to the phone and called James. I was furious. "How dare you go over my head and take this action without my permission?"

"I have proof of possession, Mother. The house is yours." He sounded cocky and self-assured.

"You have deceived me."

"The trouble is, Mother, you just don't understand. You —"

"On the contrary, James," I said. "I understand perfectly."

He'd had, in his possession all along, a bill of sale naming James Drodge, his grandfather, as owner of the property and he had chosen not to tell me for reasons I did not find acceptable. I demanded he send the document to me by courier immediately.

The next day he flew to St. John's, bringing with him the elusive bill of sale. He was very apologetic and contrite, explaining he was concerned for me and just wanted to insure the bank loan was reduced and that my house was more secure. That was his only plan.

I asked if this was the only documentation and he assured me it was. "I'll deal with this," I told him and refused to have any further discussion on the subject.

I resolved then to put aside the incident and to enjoy the few hours we had together. We dined out that evening. It was something I didn't get to do very often so I was pleased to get dressed up and so proud to walk into the restaurant with him. Angela Fowler was there and spoke to me as I went by. I didn't see her. James had to alert me to the fact that someone to my left was trying to get my attention. I introduced James to her and then to other business people around the table and after a brief chat, we took our seat by the window. I recall remarking to James that it was strange I had not seen that table of people, all of whom I knew, as I walked past. He brushed it aside, saying that I was otherwise distracted. It continued to bother me.

Good food and fine wine softened sharp memories. The subject of my retirement came up and I decided that concern for me had adversely affected his judgment. We spent the weekend together and when he left to return to Montreal, we were once more on good terms.

That week I had Angela Fowler write up a deed of conveyance, transferring ownership to Mr. Robert Joseph McCarthy and thereby making him the sole owner, absolutely, of the property at Number 5, Cuddihy Street, for the nominal fee of one dollar. I was relieved to make the decision and relinquish all claims to the property. With the new deed of conveyance in hand, I sat down and wrote a letter to Mr. McCarthy, thanking him again for his loyal service and expressing my deep regrets for the anguish that this whole affair had caused him and his family and wishing him well. I sent it by registered mail to his house.

It raised my spirits then to know that I still had within me a measure of decency.

In the end, technology was my undoing. I was in my sixties then and had little interest or aptitude for the whole process. Every day brought a new related issue: computerized spread sheets, billing, filing, catalogues. To communicate one had to be online. It was a constant parade of new aids and devices touted to make the work place more efficient. Rubbish!

It was more time consuming and demanding. Sitting with a cup of coffee, a cigarette and a good old pen and pencil was outdated. Technology was changing everything and those who chose not to join the march were becoming redundant. My self-confidence, and at times my authority, was being slowly undermined; I felt inadequate and not up to speed. It got to the point where it was more than just an irritant — it was a problem.

I did hire someone to come in and set up the new programs and applications and to train the staff to use these programs. I could appreciate their potential value, but the process of progress continued to rankle.

Seeing me struggle, James began pushing the sale of the business as the better option. In that way I could pay the bank and invest my money. That year, 1996, the year I finally sold my business, interest rates had plunged to 4.5 percent — not great, but adequate to provide me with a decent retirement income. Little did I know that it was a great rate compared to what was to follow.

Once I made the decision to sell, I was relieved. James immediately set about placing the business on the market and seeing to the outstanding loan. It seemed like a good plan so we began to move ahead. It took almost six months to finalize the sale and, as things turned out, the business was not quite as valuable as we had hoped. Eventually it was bought by one of the larger companies in town.

I now owned my house — and this time it actually was my house. I had worked for it; I had paid for it. I was no longer beholden to the Drodge family. And I had cash to invest. I looked forward to the next phase in my life, enjoying my newfound security and freedom. This time I would get it right. I was all set to live my life, without outside interference, in whatever way I chose. James and his investment adviser in Toronto prepared an investment plan that would give me a safe and secure income in my retirement. Having been my own boss for so long, I was confident that, with some guidance, I could successfully manage my time, my finances and my life.

I still avoided group activities. I kept to myself for the most part, played the odd game of bridge and tennis and went to concerts. I enjoyed my new independence. I bought myself a snappy new Audi TT, charcoal grey with luxurious brown leather upholstery, very smart indeed. I'm not quite sure why I did this or what it represented, but there it was parked in my driveway for all to see — a symbol of my success. I loved it, and together we cut a dash but there was nowhere to drive on the island. Nowhere, that is, of interest to me. Taking a ferry to the mainland meant a long drive on poor roads just to get there. I still enjoyed walking and listening to music on my walkman as I went, so buying that expensive car was a foolish choice.

As if to put my final stamp of ownership on the house and make it truly mine, I began to think of renovating. Using books on design and architecture, I drew up some plans to reflect my own needs and personality. I had large picture windows installed in my bedroom and in the adjoining rooms at the back of the house so I could enjoy the spectacular view of the harbour and downtown. In a small room off the bedroom I had the original fireplace restored and made it into a small sitting room. I moved ahead slowly, taking time with my choices, enjoying each step on the way. I was building my own personal nest.

I took to travel with enthusiasm. France had always been my country of choice. I had happy memories of my time there. I spoke the language, loved the food — I even liked their haughty ways. When April came I went to Paris. I wanted to walk again along the Champs-Élysées, to shop again in the exclusive boutiques on the Rue St. Honoré. What a treat that was! I lunched in the spring sunshine at sidewalk cafés and dined at a different restaurant every night. This was my kind of city and I inhaled its elegance and sophistication with the kind of greed that comes of prolonged deprivation. I was assuming again the image I once craved, a woman dressed to perfection, meticulously groomed — the epitome of the well-heeled traveller. I was living proof of my success. I was Sylvia Bolfe-Carter again, a mystery even to myself.

Then one sunny afternoon, the loud blaring of a horn and someone roughly grabbing me by the arm and pulling me out of the path of an oncoming car dragged me abruptly back to the present. I had narrowly escaped serious injury. I hadn't seen the car, and was left standing on the busy sidewalk alone, shaken and dishevelled, and nobody cared who I was or where I came from. It was an awakening. I had passed my first three years of retirement, catering to every whim of my foolish make-believe life.

It had all cost money, lots of money, more than I could reasonably afford. Sylvia Drodge was urging caution, warning about the danger of dipping into my capital, which was of course what I was doing. I had not run a business for twenty years without learning a few lessons.

The new millennium was around the corner and I was invited to join James and Marianne for a big celebration at their home in Toronto. It was a wonderful, elegant evening with dinner, music, dancing and a huge screen on which to watch the festivities from all over the world. When the cameras rolled into Dublin, I realized that Dublin had changed even as I had. Nelson's Column, rising high above the wide elegant boulevard of O'Connell Street — a tribute to Admiral Lord Nelson and his achievements, a grand old symbol of Georgian Dublin — was gone. Nelson had been replaced by the statue of a woman reclining in a bronze tub of bubbling water — a crude personification of the river Liffey. In an inspired moment, some local wag had appropriately christened this monstrosity, *The Floosey in the Jacuzzi*. Nelson had been blown to pieces some years previously and replaced by this vulgarity.

Nine months later, another quite different explosion, this time coming from the sky above New York City, rocked the world. As the twin towers of the World Trade Center exploded and collapsed into themselves, my own financial world felt the aftermath of the shock and began to crumble. Trading on the stock market in New York was immediately shut down in anticipation of chaos and panic selling. Five days later, when the markets reopened, shares had dropped precipitously worldwide. In New York they had dropped by a whopping fourteen percent. I was in shock. James was in a panic. Nobody knew what to do. Was there more to come, would the stock markets take a further hit? Two days later James urged me to take a loss and salvage the remains of my money while I still could. This was the advice he had been given. I couldn't afford to lose any more.

The markets did recover. Within a month things had stabilized but it was too late for me. I had cashed in my investments and taken a huge loss. My portfolio had dropped by twenty percent. On top of that, interest rates had begun to decline and continued to do so. So much for planning! My well-balanced financial strategy had collapsed as quickly and completely as the twin towers. Within four years, my income had been cut by half and my capital down by a third.

It was a very unsettling time. There was so much uncertainty about. I cancelled travel plans and reinvested my remaining money in solid blue-chip stocks, even though the income stream was very low.

Based on my experience in business I resolved to remain positive and wait for things to stabilize and bounce back. However, sharp jabs of anxiety continued to peck away at my resolve.

Then James came up with a plan that would help me make up some of my losses and still have an income. He had spoken with Maurice Duhamel, Marianne's father, about my situation. He kindly offered to introduce James to his broker — a Monsieur Tremblett who managed a hedge fund called The Sherbrook Fund. Monsieur Tremblett had been involved with the family for many years and had successfully guided them through the recent financial crisis with very few losses and had consistently managed a ten to fifteen percent return on their investments. He would arrange an introduction, but one had to be prepared to invest a minimum of $500,000. The Duhamel family was certain to know their way around the inner circles of the financial world. It seemed like a great opportunity.

With my permission, James went to Montreal to have lunch with the man. He told me later that Monsieur Tremblett was charming and forthright, impeccably dressed and very impressed by the fact that James spoke very good French. He had dealt with the family for years but was discreet in speaking of them. When James asked about the type of investments the hedge fund was involved in, he said the fund invested across a broad spectrum of asset-class shares, real-estate development, venture capital and offshore funds. "We try to identify new ventures, like Circle du Soleil, when they are in their infancy," he told James. It all sounded sensible and astute.

Monsieur Tremblett gave him his card, saying that should James wish to proceed he would be happy to be of service to the new branch of the Duhamel family. When James called to discuss the meeting with me, I must admit I balked at the idea of committing such a large amount — but after several days of reflection, I decided Maurice Duhamel would not recommend this Sherbrook Fund without being very confident, so I agreed.

You can imagine my delight when a year later my statement showed a handsome return of ten percent. Meantime my other investments were showing a modest 3.3 percent. I asked James if he could arrange for me to have $25,000 transferred to my current account so that I could have better cash flow. He discussed it with Tremblett and it was not a problem. The remaining interest would be reinvested in the fund.

I had been retired for just over five years when I was forced to admit I was having problems with my sight: bumping into things or worse, not seeing people who were right beside me was becoming an embarrassment. Driving was also causing concern. Horns sounded as I moved dangerously close to passing cars and across dividing lines. I foolishly thought they were beeping at my snazzy Audi. When on several occasions I skimmed a curb or mounted a grassy verge, I began to worry.

One night driving home after dark, I was having trouble seeing the road in front of me. Everything outside was black. It started to rain and the edge of the road disappeared. I was terrified. When two hours later I pulled into my driveway, exhausted but thankful to be home safely, I knew for sure that I had to do something.

I was aware that sometimes my eyes felt tired, but I dismissed all these signs, blaming lack of sleep, stress, even poor lighting, all of which was reasonable. I was certainly not concerned. I bought a pair of reading glasses at the drug store and was surprised to find that they were of little use.

I made an appointment to see an optometrist who referred me to a specialist. The wait time was considerable and by the time I got an appointment I knew for sure I had a problem. I was diagnosed with advanced glaucoma. Advanced! I was horrified. Aggressive laser treatment and eye drops were possibilities but the outlook was poor. Short of a miracle, I was facing total sight loss.

My immediate reaction was disbelief.

"Was there a family history?" the optometrist asked.

How was I to know? They could all be blind as bats for all I knew. "No," I answered, determined that my family situation remain my business. "But kindly explain to me, what exactly is going on."

"This is very common with this particular condition," he said. "The process is so gradual that frequently it goes unnoticed or is ignored until it is too late."

He then explained that pressure points form around one or both eyes. Over time they expand slowly, forming a kind of shutter system that gradually closes and reduces the range of vision.

"Tunnel vision and, in advanced cases, loss of night vision and blurring of the central vision are the results." When he added that I could no longer drive, I got up and left, ready to prove wrong this young whelp — and he was young, too young to be imposing such decisions on people.

When I calmed down I realized I was being unreasonable, that I was allowing emotion to get in the way of reality. So I called his office, apologized and agreed to take the treatment he prescribed and stop driving.

Nonetheless I launched into action, determined to prove myself able and hopelessly trying to postpone the inevitable.

I moved forward with a desperate resolve, booking a trip on a luxury cruise to exotic locations in the Mediterranean, like Crete and Algeria, (thinking Humphrey Bogart and *Casablanca*, I suppose) but in actual fact I gave little thought to what it was that I particularly wanted to see or do. The cruise was followed almost immediately by a trip to Prague. It became a game, a game against time — each diversion motivated by the possibility that any one trip might be my last. So like the pheasant that has been flushed by the beater from its hiding place, I rose recklessly in a foolhardy attempt to dodge the gun.

In the meantime, James, alarmed by my plans and frenetic spending, suggested I arrange for him to have limited power of attorney so he could effectively manage my accounts in my absence — or as he explained it to me, to keep my bank account topped up. Good plan, I thought. I didn't care. I was too busy distracting myself. I casually made the arrangements and made reservations to take flight again.

Christmas loomed on the horizon like a storm cloud. I have never been comfortable with the holiday so as it drew closer, I knew I had no wish to be with James and Marianne and the suffocating onslaught of parents, presents, parties, Père Noël and pity for poor Sylvia. My greatest joy now was music, where my failing sight was of least significance. On a whim, I decided to take off for Vienna and indulge myself in the feast of music that I knew to be a big part of the Christmas season in that city.

But in the absence of careful planning, I found myself stranded in a hotel halfway across the world at Christmas time, stressed beyond belief. I was angry with my travel agent, yet well aware that I had been too proud to let her know I had acute vision loss. I also knew, although I had not yet acknowledged it, that once again I was losing control of my life.

It was the concierge at my hotel who, sensing my plight, suggested I hire a car and guide to tour the city and maybe then go outside the city into the foothills of the Alps. "There is much to see and hear," he assured me, "the city is too busy at this time of year." He had a friend who could drive me and be my guide to Christmas in the mountains. It was not exactly what I had in mind, but what was the alternative? So I engaged his friend for one day.

And so I met Franz and experienced a period of awakening — a realization that all was not lost.

If you ask me now what he looked like I could not tell you, yet I can recall him perfectly. His clear, slightly high-pitched speaking voice made conversation above the noise of the car engine effortless. He was light-hearted and almost childlike in his enthusiasm and had a heartfelt love and passion for his native city and surrounds. It was a relief to be in his relaxed company and I liked him right away. My first impression was of a polite and deferential man who knew how to attend a customer — that is to say, he saw to my every need beginning with seeing me settled comfortably in the back seat with a warm blanket to wrap around my knees before driving away. His car was clean and well maintained and smelled of old leather. He spoke excellent English. On that first day he took me on a tour of the city, carefully describing in exquisite detail each attraction. He was attentive to my reactions, and careful in his responses to my questions. Even with my limited vision at the end of the day, I felt I had a wonderful sense of the city. I booked Franz for the remainder of the week. Each morning he arrived exactly on time with an itinerary planned and ready for my approval. He was a gifted raconteur, wise and sensitive with a sense of humour on the side. On day three I decided to move into the front seat to better facilitate our excellent conversation.

Franz took me down back streets and around quiet corners to the most unlikely places in his city — places that tourists never get to see. On one such occasion we visited the workshop of a candlemaker whose family had been making handcrafted candles for the great churches and cathedrals of the world for over two centuries. It was in an out-of-the-way corner of the city and as we picked our way in and out of various alley ways, Franz casually offered me his arm while telling me how the man we were about to meet was the last in the line of candlemakers in his family, and that he continued to use the same workshop and instruments used by his ancestors.

"You are about to witness the end of an era," he whispered. My senses were alive, full of the smell of hot wax, old wood, tingling to the clang of hammer on metal.

The craftsman working in the corner was in the process of applying the finishing touches to a tall, white Paschal candle. "It will be used for Easter services at the cathedral of St. Stephen, here in Vienna. It is the last one of its kind." Franz was translating for me as the man spoke.

"Bitte." The craftsman pointed to the candle.

"He invites you to touch."

I was reluctant but nonetheless reached out to the waxy surface. It was warm, faintly clinging, resisting slightly the movement of my hand. My fingers lingered and I was reminded of heavy satin on a warm, firm curve. And there it is, set in my mind's eye, locked in forever: rich, smooth and fragrant — the smell, the feel, the texture of warm, molded wax.

Franz brought me one morning to the market in Freyung so I might experience a traditional Viennese market at Christmastime. I bought two beautiful crystal stars — one for me and one for Franz. When I hang this ornament on the tree now, I can still see it catch fire in the light, visualize the rainbow of colours that shoot through the branches. It is there now in my memory, alive and beautiful. I remember Franz, too, and the wonderful gifts he gave to me.

At the end of every day it was a joy to dine alone and relive in my mind the pleasures of the day.

On our last few days together we drove into the mountains. It was Christmas Eve and with that same feeling of childlike anticipation that I had found to be so endearing, Franz told me he had one last place, dear to his heart, to show me.

We walked arm-in-arm across a hard frozen field. There was an incline and then a descent into the shelter of what seemed to be a large hollow and a gathering of people. It was late afternoon and the light was fading. Everything was a grey blur but I tried to focus my mind.

"What is this place?" I asked.

"It is the setting for a live nativity scene," he said. "It is a long-standing tradition in this rural community. The animals and the shepherd's hut are straight ahead."

He placed his hand under my elbow and edged me forward. There was a lull in the chatter of the crowd. I detected the scuffle of feet. The close warmth of the space was disturbed as the crowd opened up a path. Then the clumping sound of hooves on hard ground — the donkey passed by, its breath hoarse on the chill air. Mary, pinched and cold, sat erect, wrapped in her thin blue shawl. Joseph, unsure of his role, plodded along behind. A clear sweet voice, a woman's voice — no, a young boy's voice — interrupted my private musings. In the background, animals shifted and stamped and crowded each other. The familiar narrative began. The language and rhythms were foreign, but I understood. In the fading light, my sightless eyes saw the tableau — vivid, real, alive. And in that instant I came to realize that vision lives on in the brain and continues to exist there long after the light is gone.

"Are you happy or sad?" That kind man, who had been my companion and friend during my visit, asked me on the day I was leaving. We were in his car heading for the airport. From the corner of his ever-watchful eye he had seen my silent tears before I managed to wipe them away.

"Both," I said. The traffic whizzed past, throwing up wet snow onto the windshield. This had been a very special week. I realized that my lack of vision had never been an issue. He had painted landscapes for me with words filled with colour and emotion and love for his city, and when words failed, my senses had kicked in with a clarity and poignancy that astonished me. We had laughed and fumbled our way through a maze of experiences and he had opened my mind to possibility, to seeing things differently — and then opened it still further to reality. I had discovered resources within me that I never knew existed. He had shown me that another life awaited me.

So on that final day when I replied, "Both," I believe he understood.

So what happened to all that new-found peace and joy? Who is the cranky old woman in the chair with her grab bag of possessions and sharp tongue? I suppose the truth is that I have done little to help myself. I just sit here recalling the past. As my condition becomes more complex, I struggle both physically and psychologically with my disability. I've had some treatments and used the eye drops as directed but it has become apparent that I'm losing the battle. Mood swings are a constant as I struggle to cope with the everyday functions of life. I've had several serious mishaps and I have been advised by the doctor to seek help with organizing my house to make it safe and functional.

Before I came here I did hire a caregiver.

It is such an upset to have a complete stranger parachuted into your house. All of a sudden, that stranger is in charge of your life: your schedule, your laundry, your bedtime, every damn thing is now her domain. You become redundant.

My caregiver was a large capable woman — a no-nonsense type who immediately thought she could rule the roost. So I put her on notice that it was my house and that I intended to do and say as I pleased while she was here to assist. I then called the company and asked for a replacement, but was told that good people were hard to come by but they would keep me in mind. I knew they had no intention of changing her. I had to make do.

So, apart from the occasional ruckus, we learned to orbit each other carefully. Her name was Margaret but I privately christened her Attila.

Secretly, I was glad to have my house organized, to have Attila there to pick up after me, make tea, hand me a meal, calm me down, watch out for my safety. She turned out to be kind in her own way, but tended to treat me like a child.

"Now let's count the number of steps to the bathroom." Then she'd begin, one, two, three...

"I know how to damn well count."

"True, but the filter on that tongue of yours..."

"Damned right! I've dumped it."

She saw the funny side of these exchanges and so did I, but I tried not to let it show.

She was always trying too hard to prepare me for the inevitable and I was responding by becoming more brittle and protective of my independence. I wanted desperately to retain control even though I was becoming more dependent by the day. I had serious conversations with myself about my attitude — conversations to which I paid no attention. Lucky for me, Attila was a patient woman and was not in the least intimidated by my caustic tongue. I hope she is still available when I get out of this place.

One evening out of the blue, James called to say he was coming to visit. He wanted to be sure I was being properly cared for. It did not cross my mind that I actually might have trouble seeing him until he spoke to me from a spot somewhere by the door. I had grown used to low vision but

I was not prepared for this. I began to cry uncontrollably. He came and wrapped his arms around me and held me tightly. I cried all the harder. In that moment he reminded me of Jack, tall and strong and caring. I had not been wrapped in human warmth for such a long time, I had forgotten the feeling. He kept reassuring me, telling me that everything was under control, that I was not to worry. When I became quiet and the tears had subsided, I drew back and held him at arm's length. The blurred pinhole revealed an image I could not recognize as James. Only his voice told me that it was him.

"What on earth are you wearing, Mother?"

I began to pat my chest, my sleeve, my skirt. "I don't know." I said. "I…I can't —" and then anger swallowed the words. I wanted to run from the room. I must count one, two — and then I lifted my hand and struck him.

I struck him right across the face and from the loud smack, I knew I had found my target. And then I froze. I couldn't move.

I recall being gently guided to a chair, where I crumbled once again.

James insisted we go out for dinner that evening even though I had no wish to appear in public. He laid out some clothes for me and helped me to dress. He even helped apply my trademark lipstick and then we were ready.

"How do I look?"

"Just as usual."

"Please, speak to me as you normally do, James. How do I look?"

"Great!"

When we stepped outside, the feel of the fresh air was startling. I hadn't been out doors in a while. "Can we walk? I'd like to walk." And then as I turned I realized that in the evening light the edge of the sidewalk, the solid row of houses across the street, the pavement beneath my feet were no longer visible. They had simply disappeared. I reached for James, he was not there. I remember calling out in panic, thinking he too had vanished into thin air — that I was all alone on the street. His hand on my arm told me he was on my other side. I clutched his arm holding it in a vice grip and we set out along the street.

At first I was very tentative, looking for a safe place to put my foot down, expecting at any moment to trip on something and fall flat on my face. James didn't warn me about the step as we turned onto Prescott Street and I stumbled but he steadied me and just in time warned me of the next one. I was so nervous and frightened, feeling all the while as if I was wandering in a thick fog with no sense of where I was going or what I was doing.

This route was no longer familiar and as I struggled for control, I tried to figure out exactly where we were. We stepped down once again and crossed the road, "Gower Street," James announced, "Duckworth shortly," and then we turned right. I was concentrating so hard that I was oblivious to the noise and activity on the street, the sweet fresh air was no longer noticeable.

"We're here." James was guiding me through a doorway. I had no idea we had come so far.

When the waiter set the menu in front of me I tensed. I heard the click of a lighter as the waiter lit the candle on our table and began to list the additions to the menu. I followed the voice, asking him to repeat.

I chose the salmon, knowing that it would be easy to deal with.

Over the soft hum of conversations and the low strains of dinner music we talked in hushed tones about the success of our new investment. We were both delighted with the result. It was a Godsend. Gently, he guided the conversation around to my changing needs. "Decisions will have to be made regarding your care in the future. At sixty-four you are still a comparatively young woman so it is necessary to plan carefully. Trust me, it is better that this be considered now as opposed to later."

I asked what he had in mind and he suggested I consider giving him general power of attorney over my affairs.

"This would give me decision-making power in all aspects of your care in the future. I need to be free to make quick decisions in your interest."

I told him I would speak with my lawyer.

"No need." He had had a legal friend prepare the documentation at no charge, before he left. All I needed to do was sign.

How I wish I could take back that day, take the time to reconsider my decision and have the good sense to seek independent advice. James had not come to visit me out of concern for my welfare or, if he had, it was secondary. More specifically, he had come for my signature and I had given it to him without question. He wanted to use his power of attorney to access my money and make a quick profit. Without my knowledge he had cashed in my secure investments and placed the lot in The Sherwood Fund. He wanted to buy a cottage in Muskoka, north of Toronto, where he and Marianne could enjoy time together, instead of constantly tripping to her parents in Montreal. He needed a good deposit. It was to be a short-term loan from my account.

That was not how things had worked out. For two whole years, backed by his well-stacked money machine, he continued to deposit into my current account the amount of money that I expected to be there so I never had reason to suspect anything was amiss. At the same time he was systematically skimming off the remainder of the interest on all of my money to help pay for his own lavish lifestyle.

I knew nothing of this arrangement until he showed up unexpectedly about six weeks ago, barely able to breathe, let alone speak. Eventually he managed to blurt out that all my money was gone.

I cannot even attempt to repeat the conversation that followed. Panic scrambled my words and garbled my thought processes and speech. I fumbled around in my dark, confused world, hearing the voice but rejecting the message. I recall saying things like, "No. You cannot be serious. No, this is ridiculous," as if I was the butt of some practical joke. I may even have laughed. I cannot bear to relive the ordeal. The memory alone makes me feel faint and nauseous. James was distraught. I was frantic. When I did finally get a grip of myself I managed to find out, after repeated questioning and numerous explanations, exactly what had happened.

In short, it seems that unknown to all except the fund manager, Monsieur Tremblett, The Sherbrook Fund was under-secured. It was not worth what the annual statements showed. The fund had taken a big hit following 9/11, but he continued to pay out the expected ten percent interest that year, using money that belonged to investors like me to make interest payments.

Things did not improve in subsequent years. New money came in from eager investors and high returns of ten percent continued to be paid out. Everyone was happy and James bought his cottage, assuming a hefty mortgage.

The crunch came when an investor tried to move a large amount of cash out of the fund and Tremblett could not come up with the funds. Word got around and the façade was blown wide open. Tremblett had already bolted and the coffers were empty.

I was ruined.

My only consolation in the whole mess was that my house was secure and the deeds safe in a drawer upstairs — and that soon I would be sixty-five and have a pension. It didn't bear thinking about.

That fateful night, James, in his anguish, tried to convince me that there were bound to be residuals; small amounts of money remaining in the fund. I wanted to believe him but I knew full well that I was the "little guy" — a nobody, and in that kind of madness I knew what happened to little guys. I had neither the muscle nor the money to fight. The money was gone.

James left and went back to Toronto. I was furious with him and felt terribly betrayed but, at the same time, I worried about the consequences for him — his position, his marriage, his own financial situation. He told me he had no money invested. He was, in his own words, leveraged out. That didn't surprise me; he was clearly living beyond his means.

Now, he doesn't answer my calls and I've not heard from him for three months, not even when I fell and broke my hip. His home line is no longer in service and when I last called his office, a recording told me that he is was no longer with the firm. That was several weeks ago.

I don't know what I should do. I am so confused. I don't know what is important anymore; to find out what is going on or to cover up our misfortune. Anyway, I am too busy trying to cope with my own problems to worry about anyone else. If only I had my sight and could get about, do something. I certainly would feel more confident to deal with the issue of my sight loss and find help with my financial situation.

But I'm stuck here, shut off, dependent on others. When I think about that I become angry again and I realize how gullible I was. I then begin to blame myself. It is all too much. I feel so helpless. And stupid. I really was so stupid.

I was discharged today. The social worker has been to see me and has done an assessment of my situation. No money, no family, I suppose they must take care of me, otherwise I'll be back here again. It seems for now I will have assistance at home seven to eight hours a day. There will be ongoing assessments in the future but for now Margaret has brought me home. Thank God I still have my house. At least I have somewhere to go. The beautiful Audi TT is still in the driveway, a stern reminder of my foolishness but come to think of it, had I not bought it, that money would be gone too. So that's a bonus. Ha!

It's good to be back to my own house in my own bed, with my own things. I don't think I've understood until now how important all of this is to me. I have a home — I intend to keep it that way.

What a relief to be out of that place, to be able to walk again. I have some trouble with the stairs but I can manage with Margaret's help. I know that the government will not continue to pay her salary indefinitely and I don't have the money to do so. She has everything clean and orderly but I'm painfully aware that I must get help for myself if I'm to have even a semblance of independence in my life. Margaret has the contacts and phone numbers written down, ready for me to make the appropriate calls. I must, otherwise she may lose patience with me and leave. No doubt she's anxious to see the back of me.

I must find a way to get upstairs on my own, make something to eat, get myself to bed, get dressed and choose what to put on. I can't imagine how, but I must at least make an effort. So, I agreed to speak with a woman from the CNIB. We had a brief exchange on the phone. She asked if I had dialed her number myself.

"Of course not," I said, "it just so happens that I can barely see the phone, never mind the damn numbers. That is why I'm speaking with you." Not a good start, but the woman on the phone ignored my outburst and arranged to send someone to see me.

Gillian Barnes came yesterday at two o'clock. She got straight down to business, picking up the phone and telling me it had excellent visuals, white letters on black and a good size, but that they could be bigger. She placed small round stickers over the numbers four, five, and six. "You'll now be able to quickly identify these numbers on the touch-tone display. This is the key to finding your way on the telephone."

Sure enough my first try and there they were, right at my finger tips. I knew what was nearby. Up one space with my index finger and I had the number one, down one, I had number seven. And so on. It was easy.

"With a little practice you'll have it down pat in no time at all." She went on to explain, "It's possible to do the same with most household machines and appliances. Once you get used to it you'll adapt very quickly." She had a booklet with simple suggestions and tips, which she suggested I work on with Margaret. "Not too much at once. Safety is more important than speed."

And then Gillian Barnes said something that shocked me: "Your attitude is excellent."

Before leaving, she explained that now was the time to begin thinking about independent mobility. There were specialists available to deal with this and with other specific aspects of rehabilitation. If I wished to continue, I should call and arrange an appointment.

I had the phone mastered by the end of the day. Margaret called out numbers and I refused to stop until I had dialed ten numbers correctly in a row. Then I began working on speed. I was determined to prove myself capable of relearning how to use the telephone.

My stubbornness and determination became my allies again. I wanted to win. I learned how to organize my clothes, how to recognize items by texture or special feature: buttons, logos, collars, necklines. I learned how to organize matching outfits in the closet and to identify colours with cardboard shapes placed on hangers. There was also a Talking Colour Detector available. The techniques were basic — it was all more a matter of acceptance and a will to succeed.

Distinguishing a five from a ten dollar bill was another skill I needed and learned; folding them in a particular way, always the same way, before putting them in my wallet was a good tip but better still, a Bank Note

Reader was available that could read aloud the denomination of the bill. Coins could be identified by touch.

I began to look for other challenges. I turned my attention to the piano. I had Margaret place different stickers on the piano keys so I could find middle C, G and F sharp immediately. Picking out notes was a slow, tedious process but then one note led to another to a chord to a melody. It was just like when I had first started playing. I felt a thrill, a sense of the urge to make it work — to make it sing. And I knew I could do it. I wanted to play again.

The white cane is an essential aid, I am told, if I am to be independently mobile. This is a different story. Using a cane makes me feel old and foolish. When I mentioned this to Margaret, she told me that I need to develop a sense of humour about these things. "You got to laugh sometimes. Just pretend there is someone you don't like in the way and give 'em a whack with that cane. That'll teach 'em."

"Yes, right, laugh and fall over again, break the other hip. Very funny!" But I'm determined to keep going, I shuffled on through the house with my cane, back and forth until I could do it without thinking and Margaret all the while making wise cracks like, "You put me in mind of Charlie Chaplin!"

I am beginning to anticipate the distances, the turns, the sharp corner of the table, the door jam. If I think too much about what I'm doing I tend to lose the rhythm and pace and then I falter, so Margaret provides needed distraction. But I'm getting the hang of it. Next step, outdoors to scout the immediate neighbourhood. The very idea terrifies me.

I had the most wonderful surprise this afternoon. The doorbell rang. I guessed it was another case worker. I don't have many visitors.

I could hear Margaret's idle chatter in the hallway. It was frustrating not to know what is happening in your own home. I called out, but she ignored me. Next time, my angry tone got her attention. There was a lull in the conversation, a muffled giggle and then the sound of footsteps entering the room — slow, carefully placed steps, approaching cautiously in a wide arc. I recognized the footfall but couldn't place it. At moments like this, panic takes hold of me.

"Who's there?" I asked.

"It's me, Sylvia."

The voice and the footsteps on the oak floorboards merged and time rolled back.

"Fred. You've come back."

"I did mean to call first but —"

"No, please," I said, "I've been wondering about you."

The voice came closer — a grey moving shadow.

I tried to conjure up a picture of the man I once knew: his dark ferrety eyes, heavy black brows, the thin line of the mouth that housed a golden voice. As he came closer, I did something that surprised me. I leaned forward eagerly and reached out my hand. He took it firmly as if securing a bond. Margaret placed a chair in front of me and with his free hand he dragged it close to my side.

"No, no. You must sit right in front of me where I can see something of you," I said.

He moved the chair back to its original spot and laughed. "I'm sorry to say that age hasn't made any improvements."

"I need a sense of you, something to focus on," I said awkwardly.

"Your hair is still beautiful," he said, "more like a harvest sunset now."

"You mean less fiery."

"Yes, I suppose you could say that too."

We both laughed. I placed my other hand firmly on top of his. I wanted that moment to last.

"I am pleased to see you, Fred." I made sure there was no mistaking the sincerity in my voice. "I want to hear all about you, your work, your situation, how it came about. Everything."

He was reluctant at first but then slowly, in short, tight sentences, he began — facts only, no frills. Times had been tough. After leaving here, he had hitchhiked across the island, taken the ferry at Port aux Basques and continued on across the country with no particular destination in mind, looking for he knew not what. He ended up in Winnipeg because that was where the truck driver who had picked him up outside of Sault Ste. Marie was heading. He survived by sketching people he saw along the way and selling his work to anyone who cared to buy it. He became interested in homeless people he met on the streets and befriended many, particularly some of the native people.

"There were stories behind those eyes," he said, "real stories. I wanted to capture those stories on paper, on wood, on the inside of an empty cigarette carton, whatever I had available. I wanted, above all, to get it right, to infuse the work with the power and the truth of what I heard and saw. I also hoped they would sell."

His voice dropped as he went on to describe his work so that I had to lean closer to catch what he was saying. Through the grey mist of my blindness an impression of that familiar face appeared in a grainy circle of pale light. I moved closer, made aware of his proximity by the sound of a slight catch in his breathing. The dark intensity of his features was still apparent, but to my surprise no longer struck me as comic.

The steady rhythm of his voice held my attention. He was saying, "…then my luck changed. One day a passerby, a woman, saw my work. She asked if I had any more and could she see them."

They walked to his room and he showed her some pieces he thought she might buy. She kept asking, "Anything else?" When he eventually took from under his bed a folder of work that was meant for his eyes only, the woman became excited. She examined each one at length, asking questions all the while.

It turned out that she taught art at the University of Manitoba. She wanted him to put together a portfolio and submit it to the school. She would help him. He did as she asked, not expecting anything to come of it but the university offered him a full scholarship and he started school the following September.

And so began three years of discovery when the door to his creative mind was pushed wide open and in marched a whole new array of ideas, materials and techniques. He began to explore his ideas, to free his mind, to read, to exchange ideas — and he found to his surprise that no one thought his ideas to be strange or crazy. Gradually he began to accept that maybe he had something new and fresh to offer — something distinctly and decidedly his own.

"I was becoming aware of the vast landscape of the imagination and of what was possible. I began to fearlessly explore ideas; colour came alive, abstract forms took on new meaning and depth. Gradually my own ideas began to find a comfortable spot in my imagination," I could hear the passion in his voice as he told me this. "It was exhilarating. I was working furiously, gradually accepting a growing feeling that my art was worthy. I also quickly learned that talent was not enough."

As he continued his story, I was aware of a change in Fred. I had never heard him talk so much. He still spoke concisely and to the point but with a new feeling of assurance and confidence. He had a sense of conviction I had not heard before. Or perhaps I had never bothered to listen. Perhaps I had paid attention only when, as a last resort, I had sought his advice and he had responded with uncommon insight and perception. Then I saw a shabby, comical fellow with whom I did not wish to associate. I had a true talent living in my basement and I never noticed.

It seems he has been invited to exhibit his work at a prestigious gallery here in St. John's in April.

"I'll be back then," he said and went on to ask if I would come to the opening.

"Me?" I said.

"Yes," he said firmly.

"Even after what I did? You left the package for me and..." I searched for encouragement from the blurred image in front of me, but could not find a way to continue.

"You had seen me for what I was," he said, "a hack and a dreamer. I had to move away." I could hear him take a deep breath. "I had no plan, nowhere to go, so I hit the road." A slight pressure and I realized we were still holding hands.

"I too felt exposed," I said. "You had seen in me things that Jack could not see or refused to see: the inability to fit in, the terrible loneliness, but mostly the realization that I was cornered with no way out. This is a harsh, cruel place, Fred. I think it froze the heart in my chest, left me desolate."

"In many ways we are alike but for different reasons. I was living on the margins, depending on the charity of others, always on the outside looking in."

"But you were always included, a part of the crowd, more than I could ever have hoped for."

"I was Jack's friend. That kept the door open. And I had entertainment value. At a party I was one of the boys, I made them sing, made them laugh, made them look beyond their troubles. 'C'mon McCoy?' they'd say, 'get over here and sing.' We all have our uses, Sylvia. Jack was the best and only real friend I ever had and I admired and loved him. I wanted to be him. I wanted to be a part of his family, to learn how to be loved like him, to be smart and know instinctively how to do things."

"Do things? Like what?"

"Like sign up for a soccer team, get a summer job. Get a date with a girl. I could never find the courage to do simple things like that. He'd tell me what to do, make suggestions but I'd never follow through. It was all beyond me, or I was too insecure to try." His voice seemed far away, outside the room in another place.

"But you sang in all those shows and were a hit. Everyone thought so."

"I was in those shows because someone came to me and asked me. I never walked over to the Majestic and asked for an audition — I hung around outside until someone came looking for me. No matter how often I went through the process, I never expected to be picked. And when I was, I was always surprised. It was only once I hit the stage that I was a different person."

I listened quietly as he told me all this. Although I had always believed I had a very clear image of Fred, I realized he was only now coming into focus.

We talked then of old times and, all the while, I carefully avoided too much detail regarding my present situation. But, in his straightforward, practical way Fred asked the one vital question.

"What do you plan to do now?"

Quickly and without too much thought, I answered, "Continue as before."

"Good. I should have known you'd do that. I'll see you in April."

I'm not quite sure why I was so reluctant to seek help with my disability. One would think, from my experience in business, I would look for solutions to problems, not try to ignore them. That is what Lady Ballcock would do, but for some reason Sylvia Bolfe-Carter had shaken off the dust of years and taken over again. If I must be honest, my state of mind is partly to do with feelings of wounded pride. The very idea of walking the streets of St. John's, hanging on to someone's arm with no idea where I am or what I'm doing, is not only terrifying but humiliating. Sylvia Bolfe-Carter has no taste for humble pie.

It's interesting that when Fred, who is so familiar with my caustic tongue and quick temper, was here, none of this bitterness surfaced. Our conversation was sincere and honest. It was comforting to share my concerns and small achievements with another person who had also travelled a rough road. I'm looking forward to his return in April. I hope that he too had found the visit to be reassuring. Furthermore, he sees me as having taken control of my latest challenge. I must not let him down. I must not let myself down. If I'm to appear in public at the opening, I must do so with dignity.

I am beginning to feel I am not alone and useless. I have appointments to remember, new skills to practice or try, I even have some ideas on how to improve my quality of life. There are people interested in me and my progress and willing to help me develop a system whereby I can do things but in a different way. For instance, there is a gadget available to hang over the edge of a cup. It sounds a buzzer when the liquid is half an inch from the top. I can make tea without scalding myself!

Brenda, the mobility specialist, was here today and, as promised, took me outdoors. With her at my side, I was ready to shed my protective shell, but once I hit the sidewalk, like an old jalopy I shuddered and came to an abrupt halt. "I can't do this," I said, clutching Brenda's arm in a vice grip. She talked to me, quietly asking me to concentrate on the sounds of my neighbourhood. With that, a crow decided to announce my arrival by cawing his head off. The angry blast of a horn made me jump. The crow continued to squawk the news to anyone who cared to listen. "Oh do shut up," I shouted in his direction. Brenda laughed, a passerby laughed, I laughed. We turned and began to move away. Without thinking I began swinging my cane from side to side.

"Suppose I trip," I said

"Even sighted people trip. That's a risk we all take. Allow your cane to explore the space ahead; it gives you the heads-up when there is an obstacle in your path. Be aware of the terrain, feel any changes. As you practice you will learn to trust yourself and your instincts. It will eventually become second nature."

It takes about one-hundred and twenty hours to be able to walk independently and be fully proficient with a white cane, I'm told. It seems there are volunteers available, people willing to guide new learners or help with difficult situations. I must find a vision-mate.

I can be well on my way to proficiency when Fred returns in spring.

Margaret has been asking questions about Fred. I have no wish to discuss the matter with her but she continues to edge around the topic.

"He sort of came with the house, didn't he — like a piece of the furniture."

"What on earth do you mean?" I was annoyed that she spoke of Fred in such a familiar way.

"Well, he'd been hanging around for a nice while before he took off and nobody seems to know what the story was."

"And why should they know the story?"

"No reason really except that when your husband left and went to university in Ireland, Fred stayed on living with Jack's parents for free. He had been there for years but it did leave people wondering. That's all."

"Damned St. John's nosiness, everyone feeling entitled to knowing about everyone else's business. Seems to me that some people have too little to be concerned with? Wouldn't you agree, Margaret?"

Fred called last evening. I was surprised to hear from him. He said he wanted to say how pleased he was to see me again. He was going to write but realized someone would have to read it to me. I was grateful he had thought of that, especially in the light of Margaret's sudden interest. As far as I'm concerned, the less she knows the better. He asked how I was doing. "I'm making good progress. I have hit the streets of St. John's — a few mishaps along the way but I can take a sprightly turn around the neighbourhood accompanied by Margaret or a vision-mate."

I began to list all my newly acquired skills. He was laughing as I trundled on with my news. I went on to explain that as I gained independence, my hours with caregivers were being cut back and that worried me because I still had so much to learn. It was then Fred told me that he was moving back to St. John's to study print making at St. Michael's Print Shop.

"I'll be able to offer some help," he said.

I was taken aback, unsure if this was good or bad news. Was he expecting to move back into my basement? Deep-seated feelings of resentment surfaced and unsettled me.

Perhaps sensing the question, he said, "I've found a small apartment and will be moving in next week in time for the exhibition."

I didn't, as a friend might, show any pleasure at hearing the news. I just said, "I expect I'll see you then."

I heard the click on the other end and was not sure whether he had said good-bye. Had he misunderstood my concerns about managing on my own? Did he think I was looking for his assistance? Was that the real reason for moving back to St. John's? I knew that these were totally unreasonable assumptions. That evening, I mulled things over in my mind, trying to pinpoint the reason for my attitude. On reflection, things began to slowly reveal themselves. With the loss of my eye sight, I had learned ways to cope with practical problems but I still didn't trust my ability to judge abstract qualities like sincerity or motivation. The ability was still there: I had to learn to trust my instincts again.

My new life keeps me constantly busy. I am both mentally and physically tired at the end of the day. One of my great joys is being able to get outside again: to walk downtown with Margaret for coffee, listen to all the chatter and buzz around me. I have shamelessly eavesdropped on conversations and overheard many a shared secret. You see, I'm invisible, which is not at all as I had imagined. Nobody is in the least interested in me — and that suits me fine. People also seem to think I'm deaf too. When they speak to me they frequently shout instead of using their normal tone of voice. Even people I know do this. It bothers me; it reaffirms the fact that I am different.

Fred is back in town. He phoned right away to let me know. There was no hint of ill feeling in his voice. That was a relief. He was busy getting his place sorted out. "It won't take long," he said. "I don't have much to sort."

I did then what I should have done in the first place, told him I was happy for him and asked him where his apartment was located.

"Down the other end of New Gower on Kings Road. It's great to be home, but things have sure changed down that way. It's become gentrified — all gussied up, painted bright colours. The in-crowd live there now, not like in my day, though there are still a few people around that I knew years ago. I've invited them all to the opening."

And then he started to talk about the opening, the crowd he'd been told to expect, what a party it would be, how glad he was that I was coming. He continued to rush on, his enthusiasm gathering momentum. I had a sudden memory of a party, a birthday party — I was four, blindfolded, being spun endlessly round and round in the middle of a room and then set free to wobble about hither and tither, hands outstretched, searching blindly for someone, anyone who might put an end to this terror.

"I can't do this," I said. I can't handle crowds. Where will I sit. I won't be able to recognize people—"

There was silence on the other end of the phone.

"Fred?"

"I'm sorry," he said quietly. "I need to explain." He described the art gallery and its location, named the owner, a woman, whom I knew from my days at the board of trade. "She remembers you," he said. "There will be reserved seating available. You'll be seated next to me." He went on to assure me that I could return home immediately following the opening or stay on for a glass of wine. Either way, I would be taken care of. He'd make sure of it. "I will be going ahead of time to check that everything is in order. Perhaps we can walk together and take our time."

I'm learning how to prepare food safely, to make a simple meal. My cupboards have been organized so I can quickly identify utensils, containers, food stuffs. Since I love to cook, motivation is not a problem but it took me several weeks of training and trying and tears to manage a decent minestrone soup. I'm making progress and having fewer accidents.

Today, under Margaret's supervision, I cooked a hearty beef stew. The smell of the rich gravy is all over the house. I invited Fred to share my culinary effort. He brought wine and as we ate our meal together at the kitchen table, I told him that I'd decided to sell my car and buy a seeing-eye dog so I can be more independent. I also told him that I was thinking of contacting my brother. "He lives in Oxford. He's a professor there," I said, looking for his reaction. To my astonishment, he showed no surprise; instead he informed me that James, too, was in Oxford. He was in touch with him on Facebook. You can imagine my surprise. In the past I would have been annoyed that, unknown to me, Fred was in touch with James but now it somehow seemed natural and I was pleased — even excited. It seems James had come clean about what he had done and expressed deep regrets. "He intends to begin repayment as soon as he begins to work again."

"He might have told me that instead of you," I said.

"Time, Sylvia, time is needed for both of you. He first wants to show you that he is making strides to right the wrong. He's very determined."

"And Marianne?"

"They have separated and filed for divorce. He wants a new start. He's writing exams at present to get certification to work in England. He has applied for European citizenship. He has that right because of you."

"Is he well?"

"He's fine. He lives with your brother while studying."

I was flabbergasted. All this had been going on and I had no idea. Then again, Facebook isn't for the blind.

"I miss him, Fred. I miss Claire too. I expect the two of them are in touch. They were always close. I've missed out on so much. I'd love to see them. Could you tell them that?"

Having Fred around has been a wonderful support. He drops by or phones almost every day. He's looking for a space that will work as a studio. With the boom in St. John's, space is at a premium and expensive. I've offered him space upstairs. "The light is wonderful and I'd like the company. It would make a great studio."

For a moment, he looked doubtful. "I can't think of anything I'd like more. Do you think it would work?"

"Let's give it a try and agree to be honest with each other if it doesn't."

The next time he came he brought a wedge of Stilton — ripe and soft, begging to be eaten right away, a crusty French baguette still warm from the oven and a bottle of red wine. We made plans for the move to his new studio.

"A fire," I said, "let's have a fire." It was all so perfect and simple, what I had been missing all those years. On that particular evening, he brought news that he had been given a grant by the Arts Council to travel to Labrador. He had in mind a series of paintings on the Inuit people. "I want to observe them in whatever constitutes their 'natural environment' right now. I want to listen, talk, laugh, eat, sing — I want to find out about their sense of place."

"How exciting!" I said. "Such a wonderful opportunity." But something was troubling me, something I didn't quite understand, "Tell me what you mean when you say 'a sense of place'."

He took a deep breath and said, "My place is here. It can never be otherwise: this city, the hills and the cliffs, the ocean, the harbour. I feel the chill reality to living in this place. Nature's grip is powerful. Life here can change in an instant. When I lived on the prairies," he said, "in my imagination, I regularly walked the cliffs above St. John's. I'd stretch out on the purple heather in the shadow of Cabot Tower, hear the low rumble of the ocean, smell the fish, all the while longing for home, searching for that part of me that was missing. It's hard to explain the pull this place exerts on those who belong here."

"Go on," I urged.

"There's a small secluded wooded area, here in the east end, off Winter Avenue. As a youngster, I went there regularly. I knew every wildflower, every bird nest, every rock and stone, every patch of moss and fern. Tucked away in at the back and overgrown with weeds and vines, there was an abandoned wooden boat, listing heavily to one side, planks broken and missing, blue paint all but gone. I suppose at one time it belonged to one of the homes on Winter Avenue. The wheelhouse was still intact. That was my castle." He grinned, remembering. "In those woods there was a particular chestnut tree that produced the biggest and best chestnuts around. When properly cured and assembled they made magnificent conkers; hard, resilient weapons capable of outlasting and totally demolishing the enemy. Knowing where and when to find them and how to properly cure and produce the boss conker was a matter of pride. In the fall of the year, playing a game of conkers was something of a ritual amongst us youngsters. The season was short but the competition fierce. Everyone wanted to be king. A pug-nosed kid called Mick Reilly, from the south side, was the man to beat. Sometimes he won, but more often I did. I never knew where his supply of chestnuts came from or how he cured them. That was his secret. The chestnut tree on Winter Avenue was mine."

He made St. John's — his St. John's — sound like a magical place full of adventure. "Was Jack a part of this?" I asked.

"Yes and no. Do you remember The White Fleet, Sylvia?"

He didn't wait for an answer but began to describe the fleet of Portuguese fishing boats that arrived from time to time in St. John's. I had seen them many times and it truly was a wonderful sight to see as they came through the Narrows in full sail and then alongside, two or three abreast.

"That was the only time that Jack skipped school," he said. "He loved The White Fleet. As soon as the news was out, we'd be off over the hill, the two of us, headed down to the harbour. The harbour was the hub of the city then: the clamour and noise as the boats tied up, the fishermen calling out in their strange language, the shouting, mad to get their seabound legs on solid ground. They'd scramble ashore, leaping from boat to boat like alley cats, mad for a quick game of soccer on the harbourfront and before heading off to the Seamen's Institute on Water Street to soak away the salt and sweat of months at sea from their flesh. Something about those men fired up my imagination, the tough resilience in their faces, the sea and salt burned onto their skin, the roar of their laughter. That was where the real action was – different at different times of the year; sealers heading out in the spring, hardly a stitch of clothing to keep them warm and dry but the excitement of the hunt in their eyes and behind the excitement of hope, hope for a decent haul and a bit of cash to take home. Yes, this is my place. It's where I belong. It's in my blood, Sylvia."

This was what Fred had been up to all those years when, day after day, he'd left our house around midday. He'd been wandering the streets and hills around the city, driven by patterns set in his youth, patterns he felt compelled to follow, looking for whatever presented itself. Most of what he described, I had seen or heard about but I had passed it off as provincial and mundane, of no interest to me. Yet, listening to Fred it was captivating. I could see him, a little black-eyed lad hanging around the harbourfront all day, dreaming his dreams, lost in the maze of life and activity around him, all of it, infinitely more exciting than any schoolroom. To him it was a treasure trove. Seen with his passion and imagination it had become a rich and bountiful resource, a way to the future.

He interrupted my thoughts by asking if I understood what he meant and if I had similar feelings about place.

"Yes," I said. "I think I do, but they are not as exciting and vibrant as yours."

I heard him set down his glass and took that as a signal he was listening. I told him what I'd been thinking about recently — springtime in Ireland, about the wildflowers that bloom at that time of year and their association with my childhood. "It was my favourite time of year," I said. "Here it's difficult to find even a snowdrop shivering under the hedges before the end of March. I always feel sorry for them here. Spring is so harsh: bitter, biting winds, mounds of filthy pock-marked snow hanging around in dark corners, the ridiculous habit some people have of taking a pick and shovel to a frozen mound of snow in a futile attempt to be done with winter." He laughed at that, but otherwise made no comment, so I carried on, describing the delicate perfume of the primroses and how I dared to nibble on the flowers when Nanny wasn't looking.

I told him how the countryside around Kilgraney was all tied in with the stables and the horses. They went together. "The fields were my playground, the stables my refuge. When I was frightened or afraid I went to the stables. My refuge; like your boat, I suppose."

Fred reached over and placed a comforting hand on my arm.

"Sylvia," he said. "Have you ever thought of going home?"

"Home? That's not a word I use — so Jack used to tell me. House, home, what the hell is the difference?" I could feel old rages that I thought had passed suddenly bubbling up. "Kilgraney was a beautiful house with a name. Jack never understood this. He understood nothing of my life."

I was growing irritable and more uncomfortable by the minute. I should never have voiced my next thought but it just kept coming. I blurted that the Drodge house was no model of excellence. I should have stopped there, but instead I dug my heels in and kept going. "He made such a damned fuss about his home. Anyone would have thought it was something special. It was a chaotic place. Everything about it was shabby." I felt some satisfaction in saying it, then went on to comment on the state of the place, how his mother had no idea of order, everything was strewn about, coats piled one on top of the other on the newel post at the foot of the stairs, boots and shoes sometimes in pools of water lying in exactly the same spot where they'd been kicked off, people coming and going, "dropping in" they called it, ten things going on at the one time and nothing being completed, empty chatter, tea being brewed night, noon and morning — a ritual enshrined in that big brown crockery teapot and a collection of mismatched mugs. That was what things were like and I never wanted to be a part of it. "None of it was what I wanted or expected. I couldn't understand Jack's attachment, and he refused to ever take my side or see my point."

I looked toward Fred — so quiet, so damn laid back. "Do you understand that?"

"Yes," he said. "Not as you would like me to, I expect. Jack was my friend; to me his home was an open, welcoming place. There was always room for me."

"And why was that, Fred? Why did Jack always feel obliged to have room for you?" I sat back waiting.

"No reason, no reason at all other than that he was my friend and his family was loving and kindhearted and wanted to help me. It was as simple as that. I needed a place to live. I had no job. It was their basement or the street. Is that so hard to understand?"

The air in the room turned chilly, as if a door to the outside had just blown open. On the pretext that it was getting late, he stood and said goodnight. I didn't try to stop him nor did I get up. I left him to see himself out.

As he left the room, he turned and said, "You should go home, Sylvia, and make peace with your past."

The nerve of him. The knocker on the door jumped and came down with an almighty thump as he closed the door behind him. "Good riddance!" I muttered. I finished the wine in one gulp and was pleased to feel a sense of relief. Only later did a feeling of embarrassment and regret come over me.

A week passed and I heard nothing from Fred. I wanted to call and apologize but I didn't have a phone number. I couldn't set out to find his apartment on my own and couldn't ask Margaret without telling her the reason. I lost interest in practicing or trying new skills. I just sat in my chair all day and moped. Margaret didn't know what to make of me — and I refused to tell her.

I had just about given up hope when Fred phoned to ask if he could drop over. I waited by the front window looking out on the sidewalk so as to be close to the door. As I waited, I planned what I'd say. I'm not good at that sort of thing so I had to be ready in case I lost my nerve.

Footsteps went by from time to time and when finally they came to a stop outside the front door, I sprang into action. When I opened the door and couldn't see him, I knew I was in trouble. How could I apologize to a shadow? I had to see him. I had to see his face, his eyes. After several awkward attempts and no word from him, I reached up to be sure he was there but I was patting dead air, saying something about not meaning to hurt him, that I was ashamed and then he came to the rescue, guiding my hand to his face. I found the hollow of his cheek beneath my fingertips, the round hard socket of his eye. "No glasses, I didn't realize," I murmured. And then I said, "I shouldn't have been so outspoken. Please forgive me" — which is what I intended saying in the first place and now it sounded all wrong, like it was an afterthought. His hand was still on mine. He brought it to his lips and lightly kissed the soft pad of my thumb and said, "Sometimes, things that hurt need to be spoken out loud."

I didn't quite grasp what he was telling me but I knew he was right. I was searching, hoping for that spark of intuition that would help me to understand but I could feel the warmth of his lips on my palm and then he said, "Come with me, I have something I want to show you. Let's walk and talk. A light jacket will do."

We were about to walk out the door when I turned and went back to the hall table, pulled open the drawer and rummaged around for a lipstick. I carefully ran it over my lips. "I'm ready," I said.

We turned right outside the front door and crossed at the lights by Rawlins Cross. "Where are we off to?"

He knew that I like to track my journey, that it helps to boost my confidence, helps me to get reacquainted with my neighbourhood, so he said, "Try to work it out as we go."

Bannerman Park was on my right. My cane picked up a curb; I stopped, listened and proceeded carefully. "Circular Road," I called out like a bus driver. "Rennie's Mill River straight ahead." Then I stopped abruptly and turned to Fred. He was a couple of paces ahead of me.

"When I sell my car, I'm going to England to visit James and my brother. Maybe Claire will join us. Will you come with me, Fred? We'll go to Ireland too and we'll walk the fields and I'll show you my place. Will you come with me? Please."

"Yes," he said without hesitation. "I'll come."

We headed down arm in arm over the hill. I could hear the river; it sounded angry, turbulent.

We made a left turn onto the trail by the river. Under my feet, the terrain was bumpy and uneven. I hesitated.

"It's those filthy clumps of snow," he said.

"You're teasing me." I tightened my grip on his arm and cautiously stepped forward.

The bare bushy hedge that along the path borders a garden and beyond that, a big house. I knew where I was. The river roaring was full with spring run-off, the pounding on the rocks told me we were close to where the old mill used to stand. The millstone is still there on the other bank. The mist would be rising off the falls, drifting up to the new metal bridge across the river. Perhaps we could walk back that way, I thought. But I was being pulled in a different direction towards the hedge.

"Here," he said, kneeling down. "Come closer, you need to come closer, Sylvia, down to the ground."

He took my hand and guided it in over the damp grass and under the hedge and there they were, the first snowdrops, clusters of them, nodding their pale heads, shivering beneath the hedge, bravely spearing their way through the cold, hard dirt, struggling to find warmth and sunshine so they could reach their full bloom.

As if reading my thoughts, he said, "This one is almost there." He took my hand and placed a single flower between my fingers.

Carefully I traced the three outer petals. They had opened — a slow, guarded opening still protecting the fragile inner flower. I tipped back the downcast head — three inner petals, fragile but firm, a pale green, geometric design on the skirt and tucked away at the very center, glowing like a hot ember, the flower's life force.

I looked to where Fred was crouched, waiting and expectant. "Yes," I said. "It's coming into its full bloom. Spring is underway."

On the opening day of the exhibition, Fred was as good as his word. It was a clear, cold evening so we walked to the gallery, me holding on to his upper arm as I had been shown. I asked him to warn me of any changes in the terrain. He made no comment on my use of the cane. We just walked along quite naturally, which I found calming. As always the fresh air lifted my spirits.

When we entered the gallery, the owner rushed forward, stilettos clicking on the hardwood floor and echoing loudly in the cavernous space.

"So courageous of you to come, Sylvia."

Veiled sympathy. A great way to make one feel welcome!

Fred came to the rescue with the suggestion that he take me on a tour of the exhibition, so I took his arm and he guided me to what he considered were the most important pieces. It was interesting to hear his perspective. He talked about subject matter, colour, technique and the materials he had used. With my knowledge of his past work and the tour, I ended up with what I thought was a fair impression of what was there.

People had begun to arrive so he took me to our seats and sat down beside me.

"Okay so far?"

"Yes," I said. "Now you need to go and attend to business."

Then he said, "Try to remember, Sylvia, that sighted people are also at a disadvantage. They don't know what to do or say in a situation like this. They mean well but also need a bit of guidance." Then he got up and left.

In other words, I had to be more understanding and try to be helpful instead of snippy. I sat there trying to absorb the atmosphere, listening to the hum of voices, the occasional bursts of laughter, tuning in to interesting fragments of conversation, comments on the work, bits of gossip, news. I was beginning to feel comfortable with the hubbub when someone sat down beside me and said his name. It was the blustery fellow from that Royal Yacht; the one with the failing business, since gone under.

"Sylvia, you poor dear, so sorry to see you in this state."

"What state?" I shot back. "Am I rumpled and dishevelled, drooling at the mouth?" Then, checking myself, I laughed and said, "A front row seat is great, it tells all and hides nothing."

"Still feisty! A good sign I should think. Can I get you a glass of wine?"

"You certainly can. Thank you."

He went off and came back, placed a glass of wine in my hand and sat down ready to chat. He surprised me by being really interested in the work and told me that as a young man he had spent several summers working as a volunteer with the indigenous people in Labrador. "My parents sent me there so I might experience another side of life." He had some interesting insights to share. He thought the work was fascinating. I suggested that he speak with Fred.

"You know the artist? I've never heard of him."

"Yes," I said, "I've known Fred McCoy for years. He's a good friend of the family. My husband, Jack, and he were like brothers." It was the first time I had ever spoken proudly of Fred.

I didn't go to the after-party. In the chill air, Fred and I walked back up Prescott Street and at the top he stopped and turned me around to look back down the hill to the harbourfront and the grey bulk of Signal Hill. Way beyond there, the pitch-black expanse of ocean and sky.

"Is it a clear night, Fred?" I asked.

"It is indeed."

He stepped behind me, placed his hands on my shoulders and turned me a fraction to the left. This simple gesture of gently drawing me into his line of vision was enough to turn that moment into one of warm togetherness and allowed me to be a part of the experience.

"Have you ever noticed, Sylvia," his lips were close to my ear, "how darkness obscures everything, except the stars. The darker the night, the brighter they shine."

We turned then, his arm still resting on my shoulder, and continued on along the street towards home.

acknowledgements

My heartfelt thanks go out to the many people who shared with me their knowledge and expertise on various topics pertaining to this novel. Beth Whelan, John McNicholas and Angela Penny, Brenda McLelland, Kate Murphy, the staff at the CNIB, in particular Debbie Ryan, Jack Hillyard, Tony Evans, Alan McKinnon, Daniel Witt, Isobel Dobbin-Sears, Mark Burke, Jim Crawford, Al Felix and Tracey Dobbin. Any errors are mine.

The following people read earlier drafts of this manuscript and gave me invaluable insights and suggestions. I thank them for their generosity of spirit, for the precious gift of their time and for their encouragement and friendship: Joan Clark, Carmela Mindel, and Susan Pahl.

To the staff at Breakwater Books, my gratitude for their continued support and help, and to my editor, Leslie Vryenhoek, for her clear direction, her ability to quickly and creatively get to the nub of a problem and expertly draw from me solutions or alternative approaches. It was a pleasure to work with her.

To John and Jennifer Guy, my thanks for their warm fireside and good advice when it was most needed. And lastly to my dear family and friends who have been constant in their support in getting this book to the finish line.

Kate Evans (1943-2016) called St. John's home, but she was born and raised in Ireland. She immigrated to Canada in 1967 and moved to Newfoundland in 1969. Her first novel, *Where Old Ghosts Meet*, was shortlisted for The Margaret and John Savage First Novel Award and for the APMA Best Atlantic Published Book Award.